SHERLOCK POEMS
The Complete Adventures of Sherlock Holmes in Verse

By Chris Chan

Based on the Original Stories by Sir Arthur Conan Doyle

Illustrations by Sidney Paget

Paperback ISBN 978-1-80424-699-3
ePub ISBN 978-1-80424-700-6
PDF ISBN 978-1-80424-701-3

Published by MX Publishing
335 Princess Park Manor, Royal Drive,
London, N11 3GX
www.mxpublishing.co.uk

Cover design by Awan

As always, for my parents, Drs. Carlyle and Patricia Chan.

And for my niece, Meadow, who can't read this yet but will be able to very soon.

TABLE OF CONTENTS

Introduction   1
A Study in Scarlet   2
The Sign of Four   8
The Adventures of Sherlock Holmes
A Scandal in Bohemia   11
The Red-Headed League   14
A Case of Identity   17
The Boscombe Valley Mystery   19
The Five Orange Pips   21
The Man with the Twisted Lip   23
The Blue Carbuncle   25
The Speckled Band   27
The Engineer's Thumb   30
The Noble Bachelor   33
The Beryl Coronet   35
The Copper Beeches   37
The Memoirs of Sherlock Holmes
Silver Blaze   40
The Cardboard Box   42
The Yellow Face   45
The Stock-broker's Clerk   48
The "Gloria Scott"   50
The Musgrave Ritual   52
The Reigate Squires   55
The Crooked Man   58
The Resident Patient   60
The Greek Interpreter   62
The Naval Treaty   64
The Final Problem   67
The Hound of the Baskervilles   70
The Return of Sherlock Holmes
The Empty House   74
The Norwood Builder   76
The Dancing Men   78
The Solitary Cyclist   80
The Priory School   82
Black Peter   86

Charles Augustus Milverton   89
The Six Napoleons   93
The Three Students   95
The Golden Pince-Nez   97
The Missing Three-Quarter   99
The Abbey Grange   101
The Second Stain   103
The Valley of Fear   107
His Last Bow
Wisteria Lodge   110
The Red Circle   113
The Bruce-Partington Plans   115
The Dying Detective   119
Lady Francis Carfax   121
The Devil's Foot   123
His Last Bow   125
The Case-Book of Sherlock Holmes
The Illustrious Client   127
The Blanched Soldier   129
The Mazarin Stone   131
The Three Gables   133
The Sussex Vampire   135
The Three Garridebs   137
Thor Bridge   139
The Creeping Man   142
The Lion's Mane   144
The Veiled Lodger   146
Shoscombe Old Place   148
The Retired Colourman   150
Conclusion   153

INTRODUCTION

The adventures of Sherlock Holmes
Are here, complete, written as poems.
Sixty famous and baffling crimes
Have been transfigured into rhymes.

"It can't be done," I hear you doubt?
Just turn the page and you'll find out!
Start reading! You're in for a treat!
Let's take a trip to Baker Street!

A STUDY IN SCARLET

Doctor John Watson is a man
Just returned from Afghanistan.
A small pension, so he won't beg
And he's been wounded in the leg.

His wallet leaking like a sieve
He needs a nice cheap place to live.
John meets his old buddy Stamford.
"Know an affordable landlord?"

Stamford says, "I know someone great–
Though maybe not the best roommate.
He knows rooms out of his price range
He's Sherlock Holmes– He's smart, but strange."

"Lead me to him!" Watson declares.
They climb a flight of bleak stone stairs.
A door flies open with a pull
And bent over a lab table.

A man shouts "I've found it!" with zest.
"It works! My hemoglobin test!"
Watson says, "It's cool chemically
But does it work practically?"

This puts Sherlock's nose out of joint.
"Crime cases hinge upon this point!
You see a dark stain. Is it blood?
Or fruit? Or paint? Or rust? Or mud?

A score of killers would be jailed
If less sensitive tests hadn't failed!"
A nonplussed Watson says, "I see…
You want to share a flat with me?"

Sherlock says, "Before I concur,
You should know about my temper.
At times a moody state besets,
I play with my chemistry set,

I smoke, and play the violin."
Watson replies, "My nerves are thin.
That is why I object to rows.
I get up at ungodly hours.

And I am extremely lazy."
Holmes laughs, "Come to 221B
Baker Street tomorrow at noon!
This meeting has been opportune!"

The weeks go by, the pair begin
To get to know each other when
Watson cannot repress a smile.
Holmes doesn't know Thomas Carlyle.

Later Watson tries to discuss
The theories of Copernicus.
Holmes isn't aware, learns Watson
That the earth moves around the sun!

This ignorance gives Holmes no pain.
"I don't want that inside my brain!"
A stunned Watson feels sorely dissed
And he begins to make a list.

Of what Holmes keeps inside his mind
Here are Watson's findings, outlined.
Holmes knows naught of philosophy
And ditto for astronomy.

His knowledge of literature? Nil.
Unless it is sensational.
Political knowledge? Feeble.
But botany? Variable.

Profound knowledge of chemistry
And practical geology
He's talented musically
Yet spotty on anatomy.

Holmes is quite good at martial arts
Plus he's got tons of legal smarts.
And there's a diverse group of guests
Who come to Holmes with weird requests.

One Scotland Yarder named Lestrade
Comes often, Watson thinks it odd.
"What do you do?" Watson's restive.
"I'm a consulting detective.

I earn all of my pounds and pence
Through using deductive science.
I observe all, collect data
Synthesize, and conclusions draw."

Before more info Holmes can yield
He's called to work out in the field.
To Lauriston Gardens they go
(Gregson and Lestrade have a row.)

As soon as they walk through the door
They see a body on the floor.
No marks, no wounds, undamaged head.
But they can see at once he's dead.

But blood is spattered on the ground.
"It is the killer's, I'll be bound!
Was he moved?" "Not necessary."
"Then take him to the mortuary."

It's Enoch Drebber from Cleveland.
A woman's ring lies by his hand.
A new discovery makes skin crawl

Letters in blood upon the wall!

"R," "A," "C," "H," and "E" as well.
Lestrade shouts, "It must mean "Rachel!"
His zeal Holmes does quickly dampen.
""Rache" is "Revenge" in German."

Holmes searches with a gaze that's keen
He finds every clue at the scene.
His comments fill Watson with awe
And then Holmes makes a replica

Of the wedding ring by the stiff.
And then he theorizes, "If"
"I advertise, what will we find?"
So Watson keeps an open mind.

Holmes places a classified ad
That night an old woman is glad.
"You found my daughter's wedding ring!"
So Watson hands over the bling.

Sherlock trails behind the grandma
When he returns he says "Aha!"
She saw me behind her and ran!
She's no old lady– *That's a man!"*

The newspapers promote the case.
Into the room six young boys race
Great information gatherers
The Baker Street Irregulars!

Holmes gives instructions, out they run.
In comes a very smug Gregson.
He has arrested some poor gent.
Holmes knows the man is innocent!

"There's much more to the mystery.
Where is Drebber's secretary?

His name is Joseph Stangerson,
We have to find him quick, Watson!"

"I have found him first," Lestrade said.
"He's lying in a hotel, dead.
He was stabbed in some violent brawl
And "RACHE" is written on the wall.

His purse held eighty pounds in bills
And there's a box holding two pills."
The look on Holmes' face is sweet.
"At last! My case is now complete!"

Holmes runs some tests on the capsules
One's as harmless as a bread boule.
The other's stuffed full of poison.
Then arrives BSI Wiggins.

"We've found the cabbie you want, sir."
They show him up, Holmes is a blur.
He slaps cuffs on Jefferson Hope.
This killer cabman is no dope.

The story cuts to Utah, where…
You know, I must say I don't care
I read these for Holmes and Watson
My interest if they're not there? None.

So why waste time? Let's not be bored.
And so we all will fast-forward.
Jefferson Hope's heart skips and hops
He will confess before he pops.

Drebber took Hope's girl for his wife
This forced marriage ruined her life
She died, so did her foster dad
Hope thought revenge was to be had

Upon Drebber and Stangerson

He tracked them down, he cornered one
Drebber's face was white as a sheet
Hope cried, "Pick out a pill and eat!"

Drebber chose, Hope ate the twin
When Drebber died, Hope screamed "I win!"
At this point Hope got a nosebleed
Wrote "RACHE" with blood, then left with speed.

How crushing for Jeff Hope to find
He'd left the wedding ring behind!
The ring was held to Drebber's eyes
To remind him of his cruel lies.

When Hope caught up with Stangerson
His prey attacked, having no gun
Hope stabbed Stangerson, wrote in gore,
"That's all," Hope says, "There ain't no more."

Holmes says, "You know, I hate to nag,
But just who was that man in drag?"
Hope winks. "My friend did that smartly.
But that detail will die with me."

That isn't long, that night Hope's heart
Fails. Gregson and Lestrade look smart.
Next morning in the breakfast-nook
Watson vows, "I will write a book!

THE SIGN OF FOUR

Sherlock is suffering from ennui
He needs to solve a mystery
At stagnation his mind rebels
To test his mettle Watson tells

Holmes, "Examine my pocket-watch!"
A challenge sweet as butterscotch.
Holmes takes his magnifying glass
After two minutes says, "Alas!

This has been cleaned, there go some clues
And yet..." Sherlock quickly construes.
"This was your brother's, then your dad's
(The monogram's where hints were had.)

Your bro was careless– note the dents
Expensive watch– he had prospects
These numbers show the watch was pawned
Repeatedly, and he was fond

Of strong intoxicating drinks
(The scratches 'round the key, methinks.)
Poverty and prosperity
Alternated repeatedly

And recently your brother died
That's it," Holmes says, "You see, I tried."
This feat knocks Watson for a loop
And presently upon the stoop

Miss Mary Morston comes to call.
She's young and blonde, dainty and small.
Her father vanished years ago
And in a box tied with a bow

Are six huge pearls she has received
Annually– She'd be relieved

If Holmes and Watson would join her
To meet a secretive stranger.

"Come back tonight," Holmes says. (A blush
From Watson shows he has a crush.)
That night a coach takes them to go
Converse with Thaddeus Sholto.

He is the one who sent the gems
They were taken from diadems
Part of the Great Agra Treasure
Sholto claims his motives are pure.

Sholto and Mary's fathers both
Joined forces and then pledged their troth
To split a fortune equally.
Later Morstan died naturally

(A heart attack), Sholto worried
He'd be suspected and buried
body and loot– waited to tell
His sons until his last death-knell.

A stranger popped in through the door
And left a note: "The Sign of Four."
At last Thad's brother found the cache
Thad wants them all to split the stash.

They go to see Thad's brother Bart.
He's been killed with a poisoned dart!
No trace of treasure's found– that's bad.
The police then lock up poor Thad.

Holmes asks Watson to please hurry
And borrow the loyal hound Toby
Who can track down most any scent
The dog's nose sniffs on the cement.

Toby follows the villains' cars

With Baker Street Irregulars.
Assisting them, Holmes makes a call
The killer is Jonathan Small.

A soldier with a wooden leg
Who wanted to seize a nest-egg
A man who doesn't have much smarts
His pal's a pygmy who shoots darts.

They hop on boats, they start to chase
Small in a high-speed river race.
The dart-blower's killed in a fight
And Small goes off to jail that night.

Small was part of a robbery
Of precious jewels, eventually
Jon Small and his partners were caught
Then Major Sholto swiped the lot.

Small wanted a dishonest buck
But felt the treasure brings bad luck.
The chest is opened– there's no gems!
Stupid Small tossed them in the Thames!

At this news Watson laughs with glee.
"Miss Morstan, will you marry me?
I could not marry an heiress.
But now we might find happiness!"

Mary accepts, Watson is thrilled
His greatest wish has been fulfilled.
Sherlock groans. "I feared as much. Boo!
I cannot congratulate you."

A SCANDAL IN BOHEMIA

For Sherlock Holmes, asserts Watson
Irene Adler is *the* woman.
There's no murder here, no one's dead.
Watson is now a newlywed.

He's moved away with wife Mary
And Holmes has been solitary.
Watson visits and Holmes says "Zounds!
You've put on at least seven pounds!

You're back in practice, and your maid's
Incompetence leaves you dismayed."
His accuracy makes John swerve.
"You see, Watson, you don't observe."

Before the doctor can say more
A new client knocks on the door.
A giant, masked above the jaw
He's the King of Bohemia!

The man sitting on the royal throne
Tells Holmes, "I must see you alone!"
"No!" says Holmes, "Watson, stay a spell.
I am lost without my Boswell."

The King relents under duress
"I met the famed adventuress
Irene Adler some time ago
Dated her, didn't take it slow."

(Irene Adler's from New Jersey.
Her singing voice is quite lovely.)
"Though I was quire fond of Irene
She's not cut out to be my queen

I'm engaged to a Swede princess
Highly moral, expects no less
From me, so I dumped Miss Adler
Hell hath no fury, you'll concur.

She was so mad she hit the roof
She has a photograph as proof
Of our affair– the danger's real
The woman has a soul of steel!

Once my engagement is announced
The scandal will become pronounced
The picture will be seen by all!
Holmes, my back is against the wall!"

Holmes takes the case, he trails Irene
(He's well-disguised, so he's not seen.)
Godfrey Norton sees her often
Today he visited her, then

The two of them rushed off to church!
On the cab's back Sherlock does lurch.
In front of the chapel Holmes falls
And witnesses their nuptials!

"Before they go on honeymoon
I've got a plan I must fine-tune.
Take this smoke-bomb, please, Watson
I'll dress up like a clergyman.

I will collapse at Adler's house
She'll bring me in, and try to rouse
Me, and when she turns her back throw
This smoke-bomb straight through her window!"

It all goes exactly as planned
But Watson doesn't understand
What Holmes did, so when they walk back
Sherlock explains the planned attack.

Irene thought her house was aflame
And grabbed the photo in its frame.
Behind a panel there's a space
Now Sherlock knows her hiding-place,

Someone behind them hears them talk
And says to them, "Good night, Sherlock!"
The next day Holmes, Watson, and the King
Rush to Irene's to grab the thing.

She's gone! She took her photo, too.
The maid says, "She left this for you."
Inside's a photo of Irene
A letter says, "You're very keen.

Holmes, but I'd been warned about you
I changed my clothes, learned of your coup,
Then hurried back, cleared out my house
Then fled abroad with my new spouse.

The secret is safe, sleep easy.
The photograph will protect me."
The King's relieved, Holmes does not laugh.
Sherlock will keep her photograph.

THE RED-HEADED LEAGUE

When Watson comes, Holmes says, "Sublime!
You've arrived at the perfect time!
Meet pawnbroker Jabez Wilson
His story has not yet begun."

Jabez leans back in his armchair
"You'll notice I have Titian hair.
My assistant's Vincent Spaulding
Two months ago he cried "Ka-ching!

Mr. Wilson, you have the chance
To make a killing in finance.
This proposition should intrigue
Apply for the Red-Headed League!"

They head across town, and once there
The recruiter grabs Wilson's hair!
He tugs real hard– makes Jabez cry
"It's not a wig! You are our guy!

The League's goal is to enrich flocks
Of gentlemen with ginger locks
Come to this office every day
Four sovereigns a week is the pay

From ten till two you will withdraw
Take the *Encyclopedia
Brittanica* and copy it
Don't miss a day or you forfeit!"

Though I thought this a tad madcap
I bought some ink, also foolscap
I reached the office, shut the door
And wrote until my hand was sore.

I followed orders just as told
And every week was paid in gold

For two months I wrote of Armour,
Attica and Architecture

And I was nearly to the B's
I saw something that made me freeze
A sign! It's a puzzle unsolved–
THE RED-HEADED LEAGUE IS DISSOLVED!

I had no idea what to do
And so I hurried straight to you."
"Quite right!" said Holmes. "Sounds like my thing!
Can you describe Vincent Spaulding?"

"He's small and stout, not young in years
An acid-scar, he's got pierced ears."
"It's most bizarre," Sherlock says, "Hem!
It is quite a three-pipe problem."

They visit Jabez Wilson's shop
They meet Spaulding, and Sherlock drops
And smacks the pavement with his stick!
Holmes says, "This is a clever trick!

The fourth smartest man in London!
Did you observe his knees, Watson?
Tonight we will thwart him, we two!
And bring your revolver with you!"

That night they are joined by two men
First Scotland Yarder Jones, and then,
Banker (Merryweather's his name)
(He really misses his bridge game.)

Holmes says, "The four of us today
Will catch the criminal John Clay."
In the bank's basement, dark and cold
They sit atop big crates of gold!

After an hour, maybe more

A stone rises out of the floor!
Out of the hole John Clay does crawl,
Holmes says, "You have no chance at all!"

Clay and his pal are led away
Holmes tells Watson, "It was child's play!"
They lured Wilson out of his store
And dug a tunnel– nasty chore!

They meant to steal the gold bullion
Now they'll be tossed into the bin.
We've caught John Clay, that cunning brute!
"L'Homme c'est rien– L'oeuvre c'est tout!"""

A CASE OF IDENTITY

"Life, dear fellow," Sherlock declared
"Is much stranger than fiction."
"Actually, Holmes," Watson averred
"I can't share your conviction."

"Most mysteries, Holmes, are awfully crude,
And lack imagination."
"Forgive me, Watson, if I'm rude.
The Dundas separation

Is more surprising than you know.
It's one of my adventures.
The husband is a nice guy, though,
At meals he throws his dentures."

Miss Mary Sutherland arrives
A shy and demure young belle.
"Oh sir, I'd be the best of wives
If you'd find Hosmer Angel.

I make a hundred pounds a year
Which I share with my mother.
My stepfather too, but– oh dear!
He's young– could be my brother.

My stepdad, Mr. Windibank,
Forbade me to socialize.
I snuck out to a party swank
And met Hosmer– he's a prize!

Hosmer is shy, his voice is soft
And tinted specs he does wear.
Once he held a Bible aloft
My loyalty I did swear.

While my stepfather was away

Hosmer swept me off my feet.
We eloped– on the wedding day
He vanished from the cab seat.

Where has he gone? Please help me sir!
My passion for Hosmer burns!
No future marriage will occur
Until my true love returns!"

Holmes solves the riddle right away
He finds the solution trite.
A visit Windibank does pay
And Holmes gives him a fright.

"YOU are Hosmer Angel, you scum!
You donned a clever disguise
You craved your stepdaughter's income
And then you wooed her with lies."

"It may be so," Windibank sneers,
"But you're sharp, and you know that
If you don't let me out of here
The law would hand you your hat."

Holmes admits, "There has been no crime,
But you deserve comeuppance.
I've got a riding crop and I'm
Going to thwack your smug pants."

Windibank beats a quick retreat
And Holmes chuckles merrily
"I fear I can't expose that cheat.
Miss Mary won't believe me."

THE BOSCOMBE VALLEY MYSTERY

Our duo's latest mystery
Takes place in the Boscombe Valley
Two Aussie men are living there
John Turner's rich, he has an heir,
A daughter Alice, quite pretty
She's in love with James McCarthy
His father Charles is newly dead
Someone has whacked him on the head.

The police have accused the son
They say the weapon is his gun.
James' guilt Holmes doesn't believe
"Obvious facts often deceive!"
They meet Alice, also Lestrade
(He thinks James's behavior's odd.)
Charles wished Alice and James to wed
"John and James balked," Miss Alice said.

Sherlock wishes to question John
But he cannot– John's strength is gone.
Holmes meets James for an interview
He loves Alice, won't say "I do"
Two years past a mistake James made
He got married to a barmaid!
It's quite awkward, but there's a twist–
The barmaid is a bigamist!

Sherlock examines the crime scene
Soon the solution he does glean
"Get young Turner out of the dock!
The murder weapon is this rock
The killer's tall, limps, wears thick boots
He's left-handed, he smokes cheroots
The pen-knife in his pocket's blunt
You won't need much of a manhunt."

Lestrade is stubborn, so he balks
"You would make me a laughingstock!"
Watson says, "Tell me everything!"
Holmes says, "Trifles I'm observing,
The wound, footprints, tobacco-ash
The truth came to me in a flash
D'you know? You're a fast learner.
The murderer is John Turner!"

John Turner walks into the hall
Sherlock says to him, "I know all!"
John groans, "It's true! I admit that!
I was Black Jack of Ballarat
A highway robber, stole a lot,
Came to England, this place I bought.
McCarthy once witnessed my crime
He's blackmailed me for all this time.

He wished our kids would tie the knot,
 I struck him down, left him to rot,
I would speak to save John, you see
So now what will you do with me?'
"Sign this confession," Holmes explains.
"Soon death will end your aches and pains
If James's acquitted, all's well
Your secret I shall never tell."

Out of the room John Turner roams.
"For God's grace there goes Sherlock Holmes."

THE FIVE ORANGE PIPS

John Openshaw braves a wind-storm
To see Holmes, who's at first lukewarm
"Some awful things have come to pass!
For my late uncle Elias

Who lived for years in Florida,
But after the war did withdraw
Back to England with lots of wealth
And lived alone in perfect health.

One day a funny note he reads
Inside are five dried orange seeds
The note causes his nerves to fray
The letter is signed "KKK."

Elias gulps and turns to flee
"My sins have overtaken me!"
He left my dad his pounds and cents.
And burned a stack of documents.

Two months later my uncle's dead
Drowned in a pond behind the shed.
The police say he took his life
But my suspicions have grown rife.

My dad inherits, in a while
A note! *Put papers on sundial.*
Five pips, the letters "KKK"
My dad's found dead after a day.

Now I've received a note and pips
I'm scared I'm set to cash my chips."
"You waited too long to see me,"
Holmes sighs. "Can I help? We shall see.

You've every right to be concerned

Describe all that your uncle burned
Put your note upon the sundial
We'll set a trap– it takes some guile.

Hurry back home, be on your guard!"
The next day's news hits Sherlock hard.
John is found floating in the Thames
This violent act Sherlock condemns.

"This hurts my pride, these crimes must cease
Today I'll be my own police.
I'll capture the whole gang," Holmes bets.
"A group of ex-Confederates

Sought documents of great import
I'll cut their reign of terror short.
The assassins are on a ship
They'll be captured at end of trip."

But Sherlock's plans are blocked by fate
A gale the ship does devastate
No news of them there'll ever be
The villains have been lost at sea.

THE MAN WITH THE TWISTED LIP

When Isa Whitney, Watson's friend
Into addiction does descend
The doc tracks him to a dark den
John sees a face, then looks again.

Holmes is there in a great disguise!
Upon an enemy he spies
Holmes recruits John for his next case
Neville St. Clare's gone with no trace.

When Neville's wife went to London
She saw Neville– poof! He was gone!
She looked for him, she searched a room,
And found nothing except Hugh Boone.

Boone ekes a living begging alms
His face gives even strong men qualms.
A terrible scar twists his lip
Then Boone the cops to prison ship.

What happened to Neville St. Clare?
Holmes sits and smokes inside a chair
"I think I've been blind as a mole!
But better late than not at all!"

Holmes knows the truth, but doesn't tell
And then he goes to Hugh Boone's cell.
Holmes picks up a soaking wet sponge
And at Boone's face does Sherlock lunge.

Holmes scrubs and scrubs– Boone's scar is healed!
The face of Neville is revealed!
Boone and Neville are the same man!
Neville explains how it began.

When working at a newspaper
On an undercover caper.

St. Clare discovered begging paid
Far better than the writing trade.

Every day he'd apply makeup
And folks dropped pennies in his cup.
He quickly made a ton of dough
But his true business none could know.

So when his wife came unannounced
Back into a back room St. Clare bounced
He donned some rags, made up his face
His source of income did abase.

Neville's set free– there's been no crime!
His secret is safe for all time.
St. Clare's time as Hugh Boone is past
And Holmes and Watson grab breakfast.

THE BLUE CARBUNCLE

'Twas two days after Christmas, when on Baker Street
Doctor Watson was calling, intending to meet
Holmes, but when he arrived he discovered that
Sherlock was scrutinizing a battered hat.

The chapeau was dusty, the fabric was split.
And stains covered nearly every bit of it.
Wax spattered the top, the elastic was loose.
It was found on the street, along with a goose.

A card said the goose belonged to Henry Baker
The fowl started to foul, Holmes told the cop "Take her–
Eat it and enjoy! Make sure to roast it slow.
Meanwhile I'll examine for clues this chapeau.

It's pricey but old– he's come down in the world
Middle-aged, uses lime-cream, his grey hair is curled
He doesn't have gas-light (the wax on the brim)
And the dust? His wife clearly no longer loves him."

Into 221B a bobby does hobble
"This was inside the goose! Check out this bauble!"
The size of a bean, it twinkles like a star
The blue carbuncle of the Countess of Morcar!

Five days past at the Cosmopolitan Hotel
John Horner was charged with stealing the carbuncle.
"Did he do it?" "Don't know. To solve this odd caper
We'll find Baker with an ad in the paper!"

They purchase a fresh goose and soon Baker arrives,
He knows not of the jewel, on that they'd bet their lives.
Baker's goose was purchased from the Alpha Inn
So they hurry to Bloomsbury– time's running thin.

They talk to the landlord, they order two beers
"I bought all the geese from Covent Garden." "Cheers!"

At Breckinridge's Market they meet the salesman
His stubbornness requires a quick change of plan.

"I won't tell you where the geese are from," he says, "*nyet!*"
Sherlock shrugs. "Very well then, we'll cancel the bet."
"Bet? What bet?" the salesman queries with a frown.
"I've bet a fiver that goose was not bred in town."

"Well, you're wrong," the man snickers. "That goose was town bred."
"It's nothing of the kind." "Bet a sovereign!" he said.
"Now then, Mr. Cocksure, see this little book?
That goose came from Brixton Road, you fool! Take a look!"

Holmes lays down a coin with an air of disgust
As the pair walked away the salesman loudly cussed.
"Enough with your geese questions!" he screams, "Go away!"
The man's the Hotel Cosmopolitan's valet.

Holmes greets him, "Want to know what happened to your goose?
I know what others don't. Come with me! Vamoose!"
The man follows them home, his interest is hooked.
"The game's up, Ryder!" Holmes says. "*Your goose is cooked!*

At the sight of the carbuncle Ryder cries
"I stole it! I framed Horner!" Tears fill his eyes.
"I shoved the gem inside a big goose's mouth
But then mixed up the birds! All my plans went south!"

"God help me!" Ryder sighs with a sad mournful pout.
Sherlock throws open the door and he screams, "Get out!
A jail-bird's a jail-bird as long as he's living.
Horner is cleared! 'Tis the season of forgiving!"

THE SPECKLED BAND

At seven-fifteen Watson's slumber
Ends, in his room Holmes does lumber.
"What is it Holmes? Is it fire?"
"No, a client– Helen Stoner
Into our rooms I have shown her
My services she wants to hire."

A frightened woman, far from hale
She's dressed in black and wears a veil.
Just thirty, but her hair is streaked with grey.
"You're cold! Is there tea to give her?"
"It's not cold that makes me shiver.
Fear and terror are why I come today."

"You must not fear," Holmes does assure.
"We'll set things right, our hearts are pure.
I see you came by dog-cart and train.
That's no mys'try, I believe
Seven mud-stains are on your sleeve
Your ticket in your glove does remain."

"You are right!" says Miss Stoner.
"Sir, I can stand this strain no more,
The horror is because my fears are vague!
Doc Grimesby Roylott's my stepdad
I think he's plotting something bad
Upon my mental health the man does plague.

My mother willed a large income
Stepdad enjoys a tidy sum
But only if her daughters don't marry.
When they tie the knot they inherit
This would leave Doc Roylott desperate.
He's very strong and his anger's scary."

Two years ago my sister died
She was about to be a bride

She heard odd whistling with no known origin.
Then one wild and windy night
She howled! I nearly died of fright!
I rushed to her, heard weird whistling, and then:

My sister's last strength commanded
"Helen! It was the speckled band!"
And with these final words my sister died.
Time passed, and I found a fiancé
Creepy whistling again did play
I fear I will not live to become a bride.

And though I'm sensing certain doom,
I've moved into my sister's room
My old bedchamber is being repaired."
Holmes thinks. "Doc Roylott's a hard man.
Today we go down to Stoke Moran.
You must keep up your courage. Do not be scared!"

Scarcely has Miss Stoner left
In comes a man of massive heft
It's Doctor Grimesby Roylott and he's mad!
"My stepdaughter has been here!
Meddler! Busybody! Stay clear!
If you cross me the results will be bad!"

When Holmes cannot suppress a laugh,
A poker Roylott bends in half
And he storms out of two-twenty-one B.
Sherlock, with an enormous grin,
The fire-iron does straighten
And Holmes and Watson travel to Surrey.

So once they arrive at Stoke Moran
Holmes carefully explains his big plan.
Helen spends the night in her old room.
In the chamber Holmes and Watson wait
Staying awake (it's getting real late).
A shadow then emerges from the gloom!

"SEE IT, WATSON?" Holmes starts screaming.
Watson's not sure if he is dreaming.
Sherlock lashes at the bell-pull with his cane!
A swamp adder slithered in the room
This serpent's venom spells swift doom!
Holmes makes the snake retreat and Roylott shouts in pain!

Violence recoils upon the violent!
Roylott, bit by snake, lies silent.
Holmes takes the snake and locks it safe away.
Helen can wed
'Cause Roylott's dead
This on Holmes' conscience does not weigh.

THE ENGINEER'S THUMB

Engineer Victor Hatherley
Begs Watson, "Will you please help me?
Bandage up my hand, there's a chum.
You'll see that I have lost my thumb."

We'll skip all the gory details
From Victoria Street he hails
Victor's got plenty of get-go
But business has been awfully slow.

He narrates to Holmes and Watson
"Last night I met with a German
He said, "Repair my machine, please
And I'll pay you fifty guineas.

An hour's work fills your bankroll.
You mustn't tell a single soul.
You're just the man I should hire
Take the train to Oxfordshire."

The German's name? Lysander Stark.
When I arrived it was pitch dark.
Stark drove for an hour or so
Once there a girl told me to go.

Stark and his colleague Ferguson
Showed me where my work's to be done
A hydraulic of massive girth
Stark says it presses fuller's-earth.

I checked it out, I saw at once
Stark lied to me– I am no dunce
A massive engine, metal ore…
I asked "What's this really made for?"

That was a mistake because Stark's
Face turned immediately dark.

The machine whirred, I gave a gulp.
The ceiling would crush me to pulp!

And then I saw the walls were wood!
Threw myself through and smashed them good!
The girl who warned me grabbed my arm.
"Come quickly or you'll come to harm!"

She led me to a high window.
"You must jump out! You have to go!"
I climbed through it, I gripped the sill
Stark burst in, and he meant to kill!

He waved a cleaver, I went numb
He struck and he severed my thumb!
I plummeted onto the dirt
Save for my thumb I wasn't hurt.

I hurried back, came straight to you
Holmes and Watson, what should I do?"
Holmes checks his scrapbook, says "Oho!
This was printed a year ago!

A young man left his home at ten
And he was never seen again.
His profession was engineer
He went to work for "Stark," I fear."

Holmes locates the scene of the crime
The air is thick with soot and grime
The house has burned down to pure ash
Seems they were counterfeiting cash

The big machine with wooden joins
Was used to manufacture coins
The three other people are gone
And they have vanished with the dawn.

A morose Mr. Hatherley

Says "This business has been pretty!
I've lost a fifty-guinea fee!
And what have I gained? You tell me!"

Some advice Sherlock does dispense.
"Chalk this up to experience
Tell folks this story and you'll see
You are excellent company

Nobody will think you a bore
So do buck up, sir! *Gimme four!*"

THE NOBLE BACHELOR

The wedding of Lord St. Simon
Was the scandal of the day.
And so Holmes' *legerdemain*
Had to make it go away.

Right after the ceremony
His new bride, Hatty Doran
Having entered matrimony
Became a missing woman.

She's an American heiress
And her father struck it rich
Swinging a big pickaxe ferrous
Finding gold inside a ditch.

Just before the wedding breakfast
After the pair said "I do"
Hatty's eyes suddenly became glassed
And she stumbled on a pew.

Why Hatty disappeared later
St. Simon was in the dark
Her maid was the last to see her
Before she left for the park.

Lestrade's search has not been shoddy
He's sure Hattie is not fine.
He's been searching for her body
And he's dragged the Serpentine.

Holmes is sure he's solved the mystery
With a feat of mental chess.
These claims make Lestrade feel testy
'Cause he found her sodden dress.

"There is no Lady St. Simon,"
Holmes declares, "She is a myth."

Lestrade doesn't try to chime in
The Inspector leaves forthwith.

Then at nine o'clock that evening
Holmes throws a dinner party.
Lord St. Simon is attending
And the next guest is Hatty!

But Hatty didn't come alone
She is with Francis Moulton.
Watson's mind is totally blown
Francis is her true husband!

Years ago in America
Hat and Francis tied the knot
In further esoterica
By kidnappers Frank was caught.

Time passed with no word from Francis
Hatty gave him up for dead.
She tired of being a "Miss"
And again she thought she'd wed.

But when Francis crashed the party
Hatty's fealty was with him
'Twas no crime of Moriarty
The pair ran off on a whim.

Lord St. Simon isn't gracious
And his attitude's chilly.
Holmes says, "No criticism from us,
Let us judge him with mercy."

THE BERYL CORONET

"You think me mad?" asks Al Holder.
"I feel a hundred years older
This is a strain I cannot face
I'm looking at public disgrace.

A famous man came to my bank
"Give me a loan and you I'll thank
Collateral's easy to get
Here is the Beryl Coronet

A gold diadem, very fine
Encircled with gems– thirty-nine.
The beryls are in groups of three
Now please loan fifty grand to me."

Holder is stunned, he can't say no.
He knows the gems are not safe, though
The thought of theft turns his blood cold.
And he distrusts half his household.

Son Arthur's a disappointment
And Sir John Burnwell's a sly gent.
Holder depends on niece Mary
Arthur loves her devotedly.

That night Holder senses a threat
Arthur's holding the coronet!
"Villain! You thief! What have you done?
You've broken off three beryls, son!"

Arthur gasps, "It's still in one piece!"
"It's not! I'm calling the police!"
Father and son argue and shout
The conflict makes Mary freak out.

The police lead Arthur away
And Al Holder's nerves further fray.

If he doesn't get the gems back
His future will look awfully black.

Holmes digs around, he does his thing
Then Holder gets more news crushing.
Mary is gone, she's left a note.
"Do not search for me," the girl wrote.

"I've solved the case," says Holmes. "You did?"
"I have. Cough up four thousand quid.
"Here are the beryls, good as new
The culprit's name will disturb you.

It was *Mary* who stole the crown!
She's run off with Burnwell, that clown.
Arthur saw this, he grabbed it back
But three gems broke off with a crack."

"But why did Arthur say nothing?"
"To protect Mary's well-being.
The gems are returned, the job's done
Now apologize to your son."

THE COPPER BEECHES

Violet Hunter's worried.
She's searching for a job.
She meets Jephro Rucastle
A giant smiling slob.

"Work at our country manse
A hundred pounds a year
But before your job starts
You'll chop off all your hair."

Violet doesn't like this
She tells Rucastle "no."
He then ups the offer
And that's a lot of dough.

"Please help me, Sherlock Holmes!
I don't know what to do.
I'm seeing some red flags
But decent jobs are few."

Violet accepts the post
And gets a bad haircut.
Sherlock is uneasy
And snaps at Watson "Tut!"

"Data! Data! Data!
Can't make bricks without clay!
Data! Data! Data!
I need facts right away!"

Violet sends a message
"Please come to me at once.
Something's wrong with this job.
I feel like such a dunce."

Holmes and Watson arrive.
Violet recounts her tale.

The house Copper Beeches
Is rather like a jail.

She must wear a blue dress
And do as she is told.
She finds a coil of hair
It makes her blood run cold.

Violet explores the house
And finds an empty wing.
Trapped behind a locked door
Is some unhappy thing.

Rucastle catches her.
While Violet stands agog,
He snarls, "You snoop again,
I'll feed you to my dog."

While the owners are gone
Holmes and Watson break in.
But when they find nobody
It provokes quite a din.

When Rucastle returns
He releases his hound
It doesn't go as planned.
On *him* the canine bounds.

Rucastle lies injured
His face a deathly pall
The housekeeper arrives
And she swiftly tells all.

"Miss Alice Rucastle
The daughter of that man
Inherited money
And her dad hatched a plan.

She wanted to marry

A gentleman who called.
Daddy didn't like this
And he worried her bald.

Alice was then locked up.
To keep her from the boy
Violet was then hired
To serve as a decoy.

That night her beau arrived
And sprung her from her cell.
Then the lovebirds eloped
That's all there is to tell."

Thus was solved the mystery
Rucastle lives, a mess.
Violet becomes a teacher
And meets with great success.

SILVER BLAZE

Our duo visits the race-course
Holmes must track down a missing horse.
The trainer, John Straker, is dead.
Somebody hit him on the head.

The horse's name is Silver Blaze
He's been missing for several days.
He's set to win the Wessex Cup
And a bookie is acting up.

Fitzroy Simpson's the chief suspect
This theory Sherlock does reject.
A bloodstained knife by the body
A poor weapon– weak blade, shoddy.

With whom had the deceased man fought?
In his hand was Simpson's cravat
The stableboy's baked like a bun
Someone spiked his curried mutton!

Another clue is causing stress
Straker bought an expensive dress
Right before the end of his life
(It wasn't purchased for his wife.)

There's a long shot– Sherlock takes aim
Three sheep in the paddock are lame!
The horse's owner's getting cross
So Sherlock says to Colonel Ross

"Focus on this to solve the crime:
What the dog did in the night-time."
"The dog did nothing that night, gent."
"That's the curious incident."

The big race starts, the horses run
By the end Silver Blaze has won!
"That's not my horse!" Colonel Ross cried.
"It is," Holmes said. "He's just been dyed."

"Rub him well with spirits of wine
You'll find that Silver Blaze is fine."
"You know who killed Straker, of course?"
"Certainly, sir! *It was the horse!*
John Straker was a rotten sneak
He planned to make Silver Blaze weak
The leg muscles he'd stab and bruise
But first he practiced on the ewes.

The limping horse would lose the race
Straker bet the horse would not place
He needed money, his side piece
Loves pricy fancy clothes, *capice*?

Straker's plan was very tricky
He slipped the stableboy a mickey
Took the cravat, the fragile blade
(Your trust in him was quite betrayed.)

He slipped into the barn come dark
(The dog knew him and didn't bark.)
To avoid witnesses the boor
Led Silver Blaze onto the moor.

But when he tried to maim the steed
Silver Blaze kicked! Made Straker bleed!
This wasn't such a bad offense
The horse acted in self-defense.

The frightened equine ran away
You neighbor Silas dyed the grey
I shan't explain just why, you see.
You must grant him an amnesty."

THE CARDBOARD BOX

This really is a gruesome tale
You might want to skip it.
The story of a violent male
Who killed twice in a fit.

It starts when Holmes reads Watson's mind
(He's thinking war is bad.)
Holmes tracks John's gaze, his sights combined…
Clues aren't hard to add.

The newspaper tells a story
About Miss Susan Cushing.
She received something quite gory
A packet tied with string.

What she saw was like an assault
It left Susan in tears.
Inside a box filled with coarse salt–
Two severed human ears!

Holmes and Watson go to Croydon
Where they meet with Susan.
She says, "I want those foul ears gone!
"Don't bring them back again!"

The ears are in the outhouse shed
The box smells of coffee.
They didn't come from just *one* head.
Two victims there must be!

The box address says "S. Cushing."
Holmes has some more questions.
He says, "Please tell me everything"
O'er her protestations.

"You have two sisters, I believe?
I can see the snapshot.

And one is married, I perceive.
A steward, like as not."

"Yes, My. Holmes, you are quite right.
The middle girl's Sarah.
And Mary, with the smile so bright,
Married a mad fella.

Jim Browner is a sailor man
But he's taken to drink.
He's fought with us, away he ran,
I don't know what to think.

For a while Sarah shared their home
At Mary's inviting.
They fell out, away Jim did roam
And Mary's stopped writing."

When Holmes visits sister Sarah
A doc adds more mystique.
He says, "I must lay down the law,
"She's far too sick to speak."

Holmes then receives a telegram
And turning to Lestrade
Says, "We'll catch our man on the lam"
Before he flees abroad."

Lestrade goes to make an arrest
The culprit is Jim Browner.
Jim's angry, like a man possessed.
His confession's a downer.

He passionately loved Mary
Sarah was a bad houseguest,
She provoked fights sanguinary,
Destroying their love nest.

Jim saw Mary with some new man

His fragile psyche snapped
He killed them, cut their ears, and ran
A cardboard box he wrapped.

By only writing "*S.* Cushing"
Sue got it, not Sarah.
Holmes sighs, "This must have some meaning:
This violence and error."

THE YELLOW FACE

Were you put off by the last tale?
Of severed ears and love gone stale?
Did you find that case offending?
How'd you like a happy ending?

Most cases Sherlock takes the cake
But this time Holmes made a mistake.
His new client is Grant Munro
Grant's wife Effie was a widow.

Effie is an American
Her spouse and child died so her plan
Was to move clear across the Pond.
And of Grant Munro she got fond.

One day Effie asked Grant for cash
Grant dipped into his money stash.
He asked "What for?" She wouldn't say.
And Grant took a stroll last Monday.

He passed a cottage, saw a face,
It freaked him out! He reached the place
And knocked– he tried to say hello.
A harsh woman told him to go.

That night Grant woke up from his sleep
At three A.M.– saw Effie creep
Back in the room, she had been out.
"Where have you been?" Grant gave a shout.

Effie seemed odd– she wouldn't say.
Grant followed his wife the next day.
He saw her coming from the space
Where he had seen the yellow face.

"What are you doing here?" he shouts.
She doesn't answer, so his doubts

Increase, and so the marriage strains.
So Munro must pick Sherlock's brains.

Holmes theorizes, "In that house,
Must be Effie's *living* first spouse!
Perhaps he has some foul disease.
Let us visit Norbury, please."

That night they all approach the hut.
Effie begs, "Please keep that door shut!"
Grant bursts inside and sees– a girl!
Holmes peels her mask off with a twirl.

Grant cries, "What's the meaning of this?"
Effie sighs, "You've destroyed our bliss.
My first husband was John Hebron
A truly noble– and Black– man.

When John died Lucy was quite ill
Once she recovered, then the bill
To send her here was awfully high
I asked you for money– that's why.

Once she arrived, I hid her here
I love her so much, but I fear
The village will not think it good
A Black girl's in this neighborhood.

That's why I've been behaving sus
Now what is to become of us?"
But Grant is not a nasty fink
And Watson truly loves to think

Of his answer– "I'm not that good
A man, but dear, you really should
Have told me 'bout this little miss."
With that, he gives Lucy a kiss.

The Munro fam'ly leaves with joy

And Holmes says to Watson, "Hoo boy!
The next time I show vanity
Please kindly whisper "Norbury.""

THE STOCKBROKER'S CLERK

Listen to Holmes and don't dissent
Be careful with your employment
You *never, ever* take a job
That's offered by some random slob.

If the pay's too good to be true
It might not work out well for you.
A lonely house could be a snare
Don't let your boss chop off your hair.

Working late at night could be dumb
There is a chance you'll lose a thumb.
Bite off far more than you can chew
Will Holmes be there to rescue you?

Now heed the tale of Hall Pycroft
A young City man, smart and soft
Who worked as a stockbroker's clerk
He lost his job, and now needs work.

Just when all his savings are gone
He then luckily comes upon
A job as steady as a wall
Then Arthur Pinner comes to call.

"I hear you are a brilliant chap
I've got a job for you on tap
Please work for the Brothers Pinner
You'll make five hundred pounds a year

Plus one percent on business done
Doesn't this proposal sound fun?
Here's a hundred quid to start work
Don't tell your new boss– he's a jerk."

Pycroft's feeling like a winner
Next day Hall meets Harry Pinner

Harry has got his brother's face
They've got gold teeth in the same place!

Hall's stomach turns. His shoulders slump.
His new working place is a dump!
Something is horrifically wrong
So Holmes and Watson come along .

Harry Pinner is looking glum
He hangs himself– doesn't succumb.
Watson treats Pinner just in time
This all was a front for a crime!

A crook pretending to be Hall
Tried to make off with a huge haul
Of stocks and bonds– a bag was filled
The poor night watchman has been killed.

The phony Pycroft has been caught
The loot recovered, and he ought
To face the harshest penalty
That's why Pinner freaked out, you see.

Two brothers formed this twisted plot
One played the Pinners, but for naught
Their daring heist has been a bust!
Holmes then comments, "The result's just.

"Awfully strange human nature is!
As bad as a crook may be his
Brother still loves the vile fellow
Hall, please fetch a policeman. Go!"

THE GLORIA SCOTT

Though Sherlock loved to gain knowledge
He had just one friend in college.
Victor Trevor befriended Holmes
After his dog bit Sherlock's bones.
When Holmes visited Victor's place
Sherlock solved his very first case.
After observing Victor's Dad,
He knew that he had very bad
Memories of someone named "J.A."
(From a tattoo not burned away.)
This gave Trevor senior a shock
The old man turned as white as chalk.

Fearing he'd offended his host
Holmes planned to leave, he did almost–
A man named Hudson came to stay
(No kinship to the landlady.)
The sight of him shook Vic's father
He gulped brandy like ice water.
Holmes said "Bye!" so he could study
Texts on organic chemistry.
Two months passed, and Hudson, that slob
Got the prestigious butler job
This enraged Vic, he told his Dad
To sack the nasty, sneering cad.

Vic's Dad said, "I can't make him go,
I'm placed badly, but you shall know–"
A letter came, Dad grabbed his head
He had a stroke, was almost dead.
Vic went to Holmes, the pair rushed back
When they arrive a man in black
Informed them the old man had died
"Can you decode this note?" Vic cried.
At first the message seems absurd
But once Holmes reads every third word
It says, "Game's up! Fly for your life!

Hudson's told all– He's caused this strife."

The note's from a man named Beddoes
A fam'ly friend, and Victor shows
Holmes the last letter his Dad wrote
About dark doings on a boat.
Dad's real name is James Armitage
He stole funds, got put in a cage
And shipped halfway around the Earth
Before *Gloria Scott* reached Perth.
A gang of convicts mutinied
Killed all the guards, their one good deed
Was to let James and others go
They gave them a small boat to row.

Before the dinghy sailed away
KABOOM! A cloud of smoke, dark grey
Covered the ship– one man survived.
Hudson! The rowboat soon arrived
They pull him in, apparently
The powder sparked! Calamity!
They sail to Australia, and then,
They make their fortunes, they're rich men.
They change their names. Back to England!
Hudson returns with open hand
Blackmailed Trevor, after the stroke
He extorted the other bloke.

Did Hudson put Beddoes in ground?
Or was it t'other way around?
Whatever happened to these men?
Neither was ever seen again.

THE MUSGRAVE RITUAL

Sherlock Holmes hates to organize
His piles of papers reach the skies.
As he tidies, he finds a box
Its contents make Watson flummoxed.

Crumpled paper, a ball of string
A brass key and some metal rings
These artifacts are all traces
Of one of his earl'est cases.

His classmate Reginald Musgrave:
"Holmes, could you lend me a brainwave?
I fear that an ill wind has blown
At my ancestral home Hurlstone.

I think something has to be done
About our butler named Bronton
We hired him two decades on
He is a bit of a Don Juan.

He was engaged to the housemaid
Named Rachel Howells, but he strayed
With the gamekeeper's daughter Jane
Rachel is clearly in great pain.

Late one night when I couldn't sleep
Bronton was rifling through a heap
Of family papers– I was mad
"You're fired! Now get out, you cad!"

His voice was hoarse, could barely speak,
"Please sir, let me stay just one week!"
Three days later Bronton was gone
Soon Rachel vanished with the dawn.

We followed Rachel's tracks, and shock!
Her footprints led into the loch!

We dragged the lake and found a bag
With wire and stones in a rag.

What happened to them? Where'd they go?
Figure it out! I need to know!"
Holmes wondered where this was leading
"Where's the note Bronton was reading?"

"It was this poem with odd rhythm
It's a most strange catechism."

"Whose was it? His who is gone."
Who shall have it? Who comes anon.
Where was the sun? Over the oak.
Where's the shadow? Where the elm broke.
How was it stepped? North ten by ten
Then west, then south, then east– Amen!"

Holmes smacked his forehead with a slap
"This doggerel is a treasure-map!
We'll measure trees and shadows cast
I'll have the answer wicked fast."

They follow the instructions quick
And find a sight that makes them sick
Bronton is dead in the cellar!
Trapped in a pit– the poor feller!

How did Bronton fall in this trap?
Sherlock puts on his thinking-cap
A complex job– it needed two.
The butler called in Rachel who

Suppressed her angry displeasure
To help find this buried treasure.
She grabbed the loot, left him to die
To parts unknown the maid did fly.

Holmes hits upon a lucky break

"Show me the bag fished from the lake!"
The contents Rachel tried to drown
They are the remnants of a crown!

"T'was given to your ancestors
To protect it from violent wars
They hid it on their property
Bronton wanted it– so greedy!"

Was Bronton's death meant or pure chance?
Why did the crown stay at the manse?
And where did Rachel Howells go?
All great questions– we'll never know.

THE REIGATE SQUIRES

Watson brings Sherlock home from France.
Holmes is sick– nearly in a trance
For two months he has worked away
At least fifteen hours a day.

After all of that work there's hope–
The worst swindler in all Europe
Is vanquished and captured in shame
And all Europe sings Sherlock's name.

(A side note– don't you want to hear
About the peak of his career?
Compared to this the current case
Seems seriously slow of pace.)

While Holmes convalesces in Surrey
There is a puzzling burglary.
The Acton home has been ransacked
Some odd objects the robber packed.

A book by Pope, a ball of twine,
Cheap candlesticks, nothing that's fine
Holmes has a theory that he's guessed
But Watson orders him to rest.

Next morning, monsieurs and madames,
There's murder at the Cunningham's!
The coachman was shot through the heart
Like a shot did the burglar dart.

Despite Watson's protestation
Holmes interrupts his vacation
He studies a scrap of a note
He deduces, then grabs his coat.

To the Cunninghams he says "Hi!"
Son Alec is the younger guy

The father's first name isn't told
Watson just calls the elder "Old."

Holmes collapses from an attack
Refusing help to drive him back,
Around the house he takes a tour
He gets the father's signature.
Just when they think that Holmes is done
He makes a mess and blames Watson!
Holmes knocked over a bowl of fruit
He sneaks off and retrieves some loot.

"Help! Help! Murder!" Sherlock cries out.
They rush to him, Alec– that lout
Is choking him, his father's mad.
"Arrest the son! Also the dad!"

Holmes realized with his eyes so keen
No muddy footprints at the scene
Of the shooting, no outside man
Could have fired the shot and ran.

It had to be an inside job
It was the Cunninghams who robbed
Their neighbor– due to a dispute
They needed proof for a lawsuit.

They wanted files they could not find
The junk was stolen as a blind
When the coachman took up blackmail
They chose murder rather than jail.

Holmes knew father and son did it
To make his case he needed wit.
Because the clues weren't ample
Holmes got a handwriting sample.

He tried very hard not to gloat
When Dad's script matched the torn-up note.

Holmes solved the Reigate mystery
Through knowledge of graphology.

THE CROOKED MAN

Colonel James Barclay is found dead
He has a wound upon his head
A wooden club lies beside him
But was it the murder weapon?

Not long before the Colonel died
He had a big fight with his bride.
"You coward!" screamed Nancy, his wife.
"What can be done? Give back my life!"

Holmes is called in, he checks the scene
He spots pawprints with his eyes keen.
Not dog or cat, and not monkey
It went after the canary.

Holmes asks questions, some very good
They lead him straight to Henry Wood.
A conjurer with body maimed
"It was in this way," Wood proclaimed.

Three decades past he loved Nancy
She also struck James's fancy
So when she picked the other guy
James Barclay sent Henry to die.

Henry survived but was captured
His body was bruised and battered.
It left him twisted, badly pained.
For years in Asia he remained.

After thirty years he returned
His feelings for Nancy still burned
When he saw her, he told her all
And that's what led to James' fall.

When Henry alive James did see,
James perished of apoplexy!

What caused the head wound so tender?
James struck his head on the fender.

What animal was on the loose?
It was Henry Wood's pet mongoose!
Natural death– there's been no crime!
So ends this Holmes and Watson rhyme.

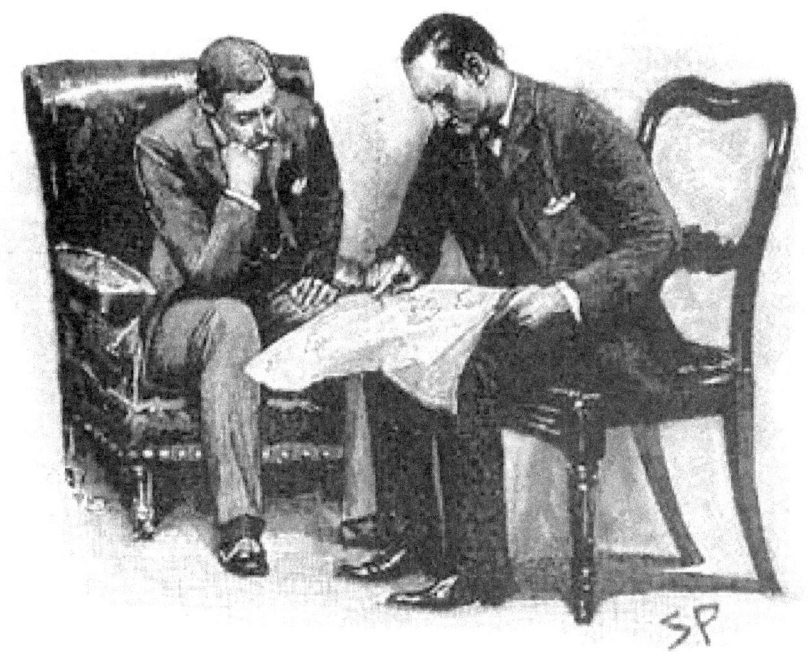

THE RESIDENT PATIENT

Starting as a doctor is tough
Percy Trevelyan had it rough
Despite being a brilliant ace
He can't afford an office space.

Then Blessington comes to his aid
A business deal Blessington made
He'll pay for all of Percy's rent
And keep seventy-five percent.

All goes well, Blessington gets rich
Percy's career is without hitch
One night a Russian dad and son
Ask help from Doctor Trevelyan.

The dad has a nasty attack
Recovery's swift, next day they're back.
Footprints cause Blessington to fume.
"Someone's been snooping in my room!"

Holmes comes and questions Blessington
Who answers not a single one.
Disgusted, out marches the sleuth
"My advice, sir, is tell the truth!"

It's clear the Russians are involved
But what they want remains unsolved.
Next morn Percy calls at first light
Blessington hanged himself last night!

Holmes finds cigars, footprints, and tools.
"Blessington was murdered, you fools!"
The two Russians, plus one more guy
Strung up the vic, left him to die.

Blessington was part of a gang
Of robbers– turned stoolie, and sang

After the others served their time
They sought revenge on snitching slime

The murderers have got away
But justice can't be held at bay
Though they gave the police the slip
A storm wrecked their getaway ship.

THE GREEK INTERPRETER

One evening while our duo dined
Holmes casually blew Watson's mind.
Sherlock mentioned in a voice soft
"I have a brother named Mycroft."

Prior to this Holmes did not give
A hint of any relative
"He is a most observant guy
And seven years older than I."

They visit Club Diogenes
Where none make noise, except to sneeze.
Mycroft greets them with stately class
And then they meet Mr. Melas.

Melas was snatched! It made him freak!
They wanted his knowledge of Greek
A threatening man named Latimer
Was poor Melas's kidnapper.

A gang of nasty villains preys
Upon a Mr. Kratides
They're trying to exploit this dude
They won't let him have any food.

They want to steal the property
Of Kratides' sister Sophy.
Kratides balks. The man says no!
At last the gang let Melas go.

Before Sherlock can find the men
The gang kidnaps Melas again!
Holmes tracks the gang down to their lair
Melas and Kratides are there!

Before the villains took a ride
They released carbon monoxide

To kill the pair– Melas is great!
But they found Kratides too late.

It seems Latimer took Sophy
Away with him to Hungary
Fret not for her! She's a smart gal!
She stabs Latimer and his pal!

Sophy has avenged her brother
And with that, there ends another
Case.

THE NAVAL TREATY

If there's a crisis Holmes always helps
When Watson gets a note from Percy Phelps,
Percy's future career's looking real dim
And Holmes sees he got a woman to transcribe for him.

A bad case of brain-fever has struck down Percy
And it's threatening his job in diplomacy.

Percy's so weak that he has to rest
Once Holmes solves a murder with a litmus test
Our duo journeys off to Waterloo
Where Percy's been convalescing for a month– no, two.

Percy's engaged to a woman whose name is Annie
Her brother Joseph Harrison meets them with glee.

Percy works in the Foreign Office
His Uncle, Lord Holdhurst, says "Be cautious."
Ten weeks past on the twenty-third of May
His uncle gave him a little roll of paper grey.

The grey roll of paper was a secret treaty
Recently made between England and Italy.

Lord Holdhurst told Percy "Copy this
Keep it locked up so nothing goes amiss"
Percy started writing– it wasn't fun
But by nine P.M. his work was only one-third done.

Percy left his desk to get a cup of coffee
When he returned there was no sign of the treaty.

Noticing the theft made Percy yelp
And no one he asked was of any help
At this news his bosses would surely frown
And Percy had himself a giant nervous breakdown

Humiliating disgrace will destroy Percy
Unless Holmes can recover the naval treaty.

Sherlock starts questioning Lord Holdhurst
The situation's bad but not the worst
No details of the so secret treaty
Have found their way to one of Great Britain's enemies
Then Holmes hears from Percy who is just barely sane
Last night he saw a burglar at his window pane.

Watson takes Percy back to London
While Holmes keeps digging 'til the case is done.
Next morning Percy is on his last legs
And Holmes gives him a surprise with his ham and eggs.

When Holmes lifts up the lid of the chafing dish
The treaty is there, granting Percy's dearest wish!

Holmes cannot resist the dramatic
And then Percy asks him to explain quick
Holmes spent the night hiding in Percy's room
As he prepares to send the villain to certain doom.

Joseph Harrison sneaks inside the room at two
And the treaty under the floorboard he withdrew.

Sherlock tackles him and cleans his clock
Seems Joseph lost a lot dabbling in stocks.
He stopped by the office and seized his chance
And he planned to make a fortune selling it to France.

Joseph hid the treaty under his bedroom floor.
But sick Percy got his room– had access no more.

Joseph's position was maddening
He tried to retrieve it but got nothing
Holmes knew the treaty was hidden somewhere
Setting up a trap for Joseph saved him wear and tear.

Sherlock warns them not to trust to Joseph's mercy
And so ends the mystery of the naval treaty.

THE FINAL PROBLEM

All good things must come to an end
Doctor Watson mourns his best friend.
He didn't want to tell this tale
But circumstances tipped the scale.

We start this tale with a flashback–
Sherlock fears an air-gun attack!
"Watson, old pal, excuse my cheek.
Let us go abroad for a week!

I'd like to relax– it can't be.
For Professor Moriarty–
A man whose name no one does hear–
T'would be the peak of my career!

To rid society of him
A man so evil, smart, and grim.
His reign of sin I wish to ebb
He's like a spider in a web.

This mayhem-causing succubus
An expert trained in calculus
His power blocks the force of law
The underworld is in his claw.

I've met my match for the first time!
He's the Napoleon of crime!
No more will he exploit London
I'll crush his organization!

I need three days, I'm nearly there
Last night at home I felt his stare
He snarled and sneered and with a scoff
He said, "I'll warn you once! Back off!"

Dear Watson, surely you must know
To threaten me is a no-go

Moriarty has got to pay!
He tried to kill me thrice today.

So pack your bags, leave quietly
Come to the Continent with me
Follow my orders to the word
Don't take cab one or two, the third

One to the Strand, don't be afraid!
Run like lightning through the Arcade
Find a small brougham, jump inside
To Victoria you will ride

Get on the train, I'll meet you there,
Goodbye, dear fellow! Please take care!"
Watson complies, the train heads east
He sees an old Italian priest.

The padre speaks, and Watson sighs.
It's Sherlock Holmes in a disguise!
"Good heavens, how you startled me!"
"Precautions are necessary.

Have you heard 'bout 221B?
They've torched it– not seriously.
Did you recognize your coachman?
T'was brother Mycroft– all my plan."

Three days they travel on the lam
Then Sherlock gets a telegram
"I might have known it! He escaped!
My goals have nearly gone pear-shaped.

The cops have captured the whole gang
Except for Moriarty! Dang!
Watson, you'd better return home
It is not safe with me to roam."

"I'm not going!" Watson says, "Bah!"

So they travel to Geneva.
One day they go out for a walk
To see the falls of Reichenbach.

Watson's called back: "Emergency!"
He hurries back, only to see
It was a hoax! He runs to Holmes!
There's no one near Reichenbach's foams.

He spots a note under a stone
It says, "Dear Watson, I have known
Moriarty has come to duel
He's mad as hell, his soul is cruel,

We two will fight, I wonder if
We both shall fall right off the cliff!"
Examination of the scene
Proves that is what happened between

Holmes and the prof, they fought, they fell
There really is no more to tell.
Watson mourns his pal with a moan.
"The best and wisest man I've known."

THE HOUND OF THE BASKERVILLES

Note: This tale of fear and mayhem
Is set before "Final Problem."

One morning at Two-Two-One-B, a walking stick Watson studies,
While the pair were out somebody left it behind the night before–
"Well?" Holmes asks with sparkling wit, "Watson, what do you make of it?"
John studies the cane bit by bit, every clue accounted for,
"This odd visitor," John infers, "Is the man James Mortimer–[*]
The man's profession is doctor."

"The doc's a man of advanced years, well-esteemed by all of his peers,
He must live in bucolic spheres– cane's from eighteen-eighty four.
"C.C.H.?" Watson gives a grunt– "Stands for the something something Hunt!"
"Sorry, Watson," Holmes is blunt– "I give you a failing score
Your deductions are all faulty– Listen to me, don't get sore!
I'll point out your first error.

Your face should not be all that long, you were not altogether wrong.
True, he likes to walk a furlong– in the country furthermore.
If my reas'ning is judicious, this fellow is not ambitious
And it's further supposititious that he's younger than two score
C.C.H.– "Charing Cross Hospital" better fits a doctor
Ah! He's returned to our door!"

Enter a young, jovial fellow– friendly, obsessed with skulls, mellow
Pulls out a manuscript yellow, 'tis Baskerville fam'ly lore.
"Here's a legend that I have found, 'bout a supernatural hound
Stalking over Baskerville ground, haunting a great swath of moor."
Holmes finds this entire story one great big enormous bore.
He doesn't care anymore.

―――――――――――――

[*] Dear reader, please do me a favor and for the purposes of this poem, pronounce it "Morti–MORE." In other cases, a bit of similar stretching would also be appreciated.

James observes Holmes' interest chill, and explains Sir Charles Baskerville
A massive heart attack did kill before he saw the doctor.
Down the alley Charles was walking, he must have seen something shocking
So scared that his knees were knocking, and he collapsed on the floor.
Had a heart attack that left him as dead as a stegosaur.
"Wait, Mr. Holmes! There is more!

By the body, scattered around, were the footprints of a huge hound!"
Watson's mouth is open and round, Holmes' interest does restore
"Young Sir Henry is the new heir, and I fear the curse will not spare
The man– he doesn't have a prayer, unless, Holmes you can explore
And discover the truth behind what caused this Gothic horror."
Holmes agrees with real fervor.

Sir Henry comes on the morrow, "Holmes, I know your work is thorough."
"Have you a boot I can borrow? One of mine's vanished like vapor.
Boy, does that really get my goat. By the way, I've received this note"
In cut-and-pasted words is wrote a threat that I can't ignore.
AS YOU VALUE YOUR LIFE AND REASON KEEP AWAY FROM THE MOOR!
"I will save you," Sherlock swore.

After some more misadventures, Holmes sends John solo to the moors
"I'll be very glad," Holmes assures, "when you're safe at home once more."
Watson and pals start to travel, coach wheels turn upon the gravel
Hope the villain's plans unravel, otherwise Henry's done for.
Then they learn the convict Selden is hiding upon the moor.
The Notting Hill Murderer.

They arrive at Baskerville Hall, dull light and fog leave a grim pall,
"Welcome, Sir Henry!" comes a call. It is the butler, Barrymore.
Leaving servants to their labors, Henry and John meet the neighbors.
"Jack Stapleton! What's mine is yours! Can I give you two a tour?
That's the Great Grimpen Mire, take one false step, your odds are poor.

Please be careful, I implore."

Then a lady comes to Watson, 'tis the sister, Miss Stapleton
"Leave this place, go back to London," Beryl hisses with ardor.
Then Sir Henry falls for Beryl, that makes her brother turn feral
Tensions rise, a sense of peril, John looks down the corridor
With a candle at the window is the butler Barrymore
What is he doing that for?

Stapleton's still behaving sus, and the butler's actions nonplus
Plans Watson and Henry discuss, they will spy on Barrymore
They're up late although they're tired, butler's response uninspired
"Tell the truth or you are fired!" Enter Mrs. Barrymore.
"Convict Selden is my brother hiding out upon the moor!"
She sobs in her pinafore.

She can't bear to send him to jail, though his actions beyond the pale.
Henry's efforts to catch him fail. "Here's a clue" says Barrymore.
"Though what it means I cannot tell, Sir Charles got a note signed "L.L"
Laura Lyons! It's a bombshell– John tries not to be a boor.
Lyons claims she has no idea what happened upon the moor
There's a man upon the tor.

Watson goes to investigate, sets a trap with himself as bait
Sits in a hut and forced to wait, holds his service revolver.
The mysterious man comes back, Watson prepares for an attack
Just then a familiar voice spake, "Lovely evening, dear doctor
I think you will be more comfortable if you go outdoor."
Sherlock Holmes is on the moor!

Watson cannot believe this twist, his protestations are dismissed
Watson's long reports were not missed, over them Sherlock did pore.
Stapleton's a twisted mister, Beryl's his wife, not his sister.
"Jack's our villain!" Holmes does whisper, "He's scum– pardon my candor.
I will bring down Stapleton just like the wizard Dumbledore
Would battle Lord Voldemort."

First a scream, then a sick'ning thud, Holmes and John run across the mud,
Find a body lying in blood, 'Tis Henry covered in gore!
Holmes notices something weird– the dead body has a beard!
It's not Sir Henry as they feared! 'Tis the convict they searched for!
Wearing Henry's clothes provided by his in-law Barrymore.
Jack has much to answer for.

Time this story reached its climax, Holmes and Watson say they'll make tracks,
"Don't you worry, we will be back," Holmes is Henry's guarantor.
They'll resolve this imbroglio, Lestrade comes and makes a trio
Suddenly a figure aglow appears and runs 'cross the moor!
The Hound of the Baskervilles attacks Sir Henry! Poor señor!
Watson aims his revolver.

Sherlock also fires his gun, hits the hound, kills it, and it's done.
It looks like the good guys have won this unsettling little war.
Henry's wounded but he'll be fine, Sherlock then inspects the canine:
Though it gives off ghoulish shine, and it's big as a wild boar
'Tis no specter but simply a large doggie dipped in phosphor!
Stapleton they must look for.

When they search at Stapleton's house, they find that he's tied up his spouse.
Boy is she mad! "That dirty louse! He's run off across the moor!
The remains of a tin mine are where you'll find that filthy liar!
He'll be hiding in the mire, the darned human cuspidor!"
Before they catch Stapleton he slips and falls in muck impure!
Will he emerge? Nevermore!

Sherlock then explains to Watson, Stapleton is Henry's cousin.
If Jack's plot was successful then Jack would be inheritor
First the Hound chased Sir Charles to death, stalked Henry with fetid breath.
"Elementary!" (his shibboleth)– "That was his cruel plot's wherefore!"
This is their biggest adventure since they solved *The Sign of Four*.
The pair's plans? An opera score!

THE EMPTY HOUSE

Was that truly the end? Oh, no!
There's still half of this book to go!
Take heart, Sherlock Holmes fans! Stay strong!
Our man cannot stay dead for long!

At story's start, Watson's life's dim
It's a very sad time for him.
His wife Mary has passed away
He doesn't want to work or play.

But fate for him has grand designs
A murder takes up the headlines
A young card-sharp, Ronald Adair
Received a bullet through his hair.

Watson sighs, "I can't help, I fear
If only Sherlock Holmes was here!"
The thought of Holmes gives Watson tears
Then an old bookseller appears.

The peddler says, "Please buy a book!"
Watson turns his head round to look
At his bookshelf, then he espies
The peddler's removed his disguise!

Holmes is alive! "How are you, bud?"
Watson hits the floor with a thud.
Sherlock revives him. "You okay?"
"Yes! How'd you survive the melee?"

"I never fell into the Falls
I have survived my share of brawls.
The prof attacked– in self-defense
I shoved him off the cliff, and thence

I climbed the cliff, I took a breath
I convincingly faked my death.
A villain boulders at me hurled
I ran away and saw the world.

First went to Florence, then Tibet
Then Persia, Mecca, Sudan, yet!
I studied coal-tar in South France
Then by a lucky circumstance.

I learned that of all the prof's gang
Only one from law's clutches sprang.
I hurried back to catch that lout
(My face freaked Mrs. Hudson out.)

You find my secrecy uncouth
Only my brother knew the truth
Please don't think me a selfish jerk.
The best cure for sorrow is work!"

The two make up, and presently
'Cross the street from 221B
They sit and wait, and soon they find
Silhouetted upon the blind

Holmes' profile! It's a wax bust.
Watson finds the trick marvelous
When midnight strikes, they hear a shot!
A struggle, and the villain's caught!

The guy is the prof's right-hand man
It's Colonel Sebastian Moran
He looks at Holmes with a death-glare
(He also shot Ronald Adair.)

Back in their rooms, Sherlock explains
Moran's no match for Holmes' brains
It was a clumsy planned attack.
AT LONG LAST SHERLOCK HOLMES IS BACK!

THE NORWOOD BUILDER

"Please help, Holmes!" John McFarlane said.
"My position's not funny.
My client's missing, presumed dead
He's left me all his money.

Jonas Oldacre's will I drew
He told me to tell no one.
Next day news said his life was through
And so I went on the run."

At the door Lestrade comes knocking
He's come to make an arrest
"To a prison cell you're walking"
McFarlane is clearly stressed.

Holmes visits McFarland's mother
Seems Oldacre was a louse.
They were engaged to each other
'Til she chose a better spouse.

After searching Oldacre's home
Holmes hears more from Scotland Yard.
They've got some clues that are noisome
Buttons and bones were found charred.

But the proof of McFarlane's guilt
Is a thumbprint on the wall
Left in blood that the victim spilt
Now Lestrade is standing tall.

Lestrade's insufferably smug
"There's nothing that you can do.
I've solved the case, I've caught the thug
So nanny nanny boo boo."

Holmes then bursts into hysterics
Has the great detective flipped?

No! Holmes knows someone's up to tricks.
For he sees things nondescript.

The thumbprint was not there before!
Holmes will testify to that.
He piles straw on Oldacre's floor
And pours water in a vat.

Then he sets the straw afire
And it makes a lot of smoke
Out comes Oldacre– that liar!
He claims it was all a joke.

Hiding in a secret chamber
Oldacre plotted payback.
His ex? He never forgave her.
He framed her son. Maniac!

Out to trap Ma McFarlane's son.
Stamped a wax print on the wall.
"He tried to improve perfection
So Oldacre ruined all."

THE DANCING MEN

We open with a classic scene:
Holmes studies Watson with eyes keen
And from chalk dust and no checkbook
Knows an investment didn't hook.

Then Hilton Cubitt comes to call
Stick-figures were drawn on his wall
They caused his wife Elsie to freak
More stick-figures came the next week.

Elsie knows more than she will say
Hilton respects her privacy.
The dancing men Sherlock is showed
And patiently he cracks the code.

Holmes rushes off to see Cubitt
But he's too late– there's an obit
Cubitt was shot and killed that night
And Elsie's wounded– it's not slight.

The gun was found between the two
And the police are wond'ring who
Shot first – did she shoot him, then her?
Was Hilton the first to fire?

Holmes hunts for clues and presently
He writes a note to Abe Slaney
He's staying at a nearby farm
And he's the one who did this harm.

Slaney arrives, "Hello?" he said
Holmes claps a pistol to his head.
Responding to questions Slaney
Says he was engaged to Elsie.

Of him Elsie was not so fond
She ran away across the pond

He tracked her down to get her back
And that led straight to the attack.

When he tried to kidnap Elsie
He shot Hilton and tried to flee
Her husband's death left Elsie beat
And so she tried to self-delete.

Slaney was lured with a flim-flam
The dancing men's a cryptogram
Sherlock, you see, determined this
Through frequency analysis.

The cops arrest the Slaney dude
And he gets penal servitude
Elsie recovers totally
Devotes her life to charity.

THE SOLITARY CYCLIST

Miss Violet Smith teaches music
She needs some help and needs it quick
Her father's dead, her mother's broke
And then they meet a pair of blokes.

Mr. Carruthers' nice enough.
Mr. Woodley's manners are rough.
Late Uncle Ralph's a pal of theirs
Before he died Ralph showed he cares.

Violet wants a music career
So for a hundred pounds a year
She'll teach Carruthers' kid music
But Woodley's lusts make Violet sick.

When Violet rides upon her bike
She sees something she doesn't like
A man with a giant black beard
Follows behind– it's really weird.

Holmes and Watson investigate
Holmes says John's tactics aren't great
When Sherlock asked what Woodley knows
Woodley and Sherlock came to blows.

When someone takes Violet away
Our duo comes to save the day
They soon meet the bearded cyclist
He wants to help them– what a twist!

They follow the trail to a grove
A wedding's there– not based on love.
Woodley's the groom, he's smiling wide
Violet's a most reluctant bride.

The officiant's been defrocked
"You're too late!" Mr. Woodley mocked.

The cyclist then rips off his beard
It's Carruthers! Then Woodley sneered.

"She's my wife!" laughs the nasty sot
Carruthers pulls a gun. "She's not!"
"She's your widow!" He fires once.
Holmes snaps, "Drop that pistol, you dunce!"

"The wedding's not legitimate
You didn't have to shoot, you twit.
A forced marriage's not real, you see,
It's a serious felony."

Woodley's wounded, but he will live
Now answers Carruthers must give
Though Woodley warns him not to snitch
He says Uncle Ralph was quite rich.

Violet inherits tons of loot
And Woodley, that disgusting brute
Sought to wed her and get the dough
Carruthers, who loved her, said "no."

Violet is saved! Let's give a cheer!
She then marries an engineer
Woodley's convicted– sent to jail
And that is the end of this tale.

THE PRIORY SCHOOL

Doctor Thorneycroft Huxtable
Collapses like a big sack full
Of potatoes pompous and smug
Upon Holmes' bearskin hearth-rug.

When he revives, Huxtable pleads
"My career's going in the reeds!"
"We're very busy…" Holmes replies.
"It's important!" Huxtable cries.

"My school could be crushed by the mess
Because the Duke of Holdernesse–
(The greatest subject of the Crown!)
Took his son to my school renowned.

Young Lord Saltire's disappeared!
The German master Heidegger
Is also gone without a trace
So Holmes, you have to take the case!"

Sherlock listens and then frowns. "Hmm!
Why did you wait three days to come?"
"The cops were thought fit to handle
The case and to prevent scandal.

The Duke's utterly adamant
Can't have publicity! He can't!"
So Holmes and Watson pay their fare
And try to find the missing heir.

When they arrive at the Duke's place
The Duke has a most pallid face.
James Wilder, his secretary,
Says, "You shouldn't have called Holmes, you flea!"

Holmes snaps at him "What tommyrot!
You want to find your son or not?

Further delay could end his life
Unless it was your estranged wife?"

The Duke says, "I've told the police
To focus on the town of Nice
In Southern France, it's where my spouse
Has got a most impressive house.

I'm sure my boy and his teacher
Travelled down to France to see her
The police's work I commend
This interview is at an end."

And though the time is running late
Holmes begins to investigate
He trails bike tracks to a morass
Heidegger's dead upon the grass.

It's murder done with a bludgeon!
Holmes hurries to a squalid inn
And meets the owner Reuben Hayes
For the Duke Reuben has no praise.

Holmes asks Watson, "Didn't you see
That in the mud there were many
Cow-tracks, but can you tell me how
We didn't see a single cow?

"It is remarkable," Holmes talks,
"A cow that gallops, skips and walks."
They poke around the inn's stable
Hayes says something condemnable.

They leave the inn (The Fighting Cock.)
A familiar face shocks Sherlock
It's Wilder– he does not look good
He meets a man wearing a hood.

Next morning the pair ring the bell

Wilder says, "My master's not well."
Holmes' voice is as cold as doom
"Then I shall go to his bedroom."

The Duke is looking weak and dun
"Mr. Holmes, have you found my son?"
"Which son are you referring to?"
Holmes asks. "One of them's next to you!"

Wilder's face blanches to his hair
He is the child of an affair
That the Duke had during his youth
(To give details would be uncouth.)

Jealousy caused Wilder to hate
Wished to be heir of the estate
So he kidnapped his half-sibling
But fate is quite a fickle thing.

Wilder had partnered up with Hayes.
The innkeeper's mind was half-crazed.
He beat Heidegger dead, although
This detail Wilder didn't know.

Duke says, "I learned the truth last night.
I know what I've done isn't right.
Wilder begged me to let Hayes run
And soon I would get back my son."

Sherlock's censorious and cool.
"You've acted like a bloody fool.
You cannot trust this wicked man
But I will fix things if I can."

Holmes tells the butler "Fetch the boy!
So to the Fighting Cock deploy!
And as for the killer Hayes? Faugh!
He'll face the power of the law.

He is an angry, greedy chap.
Pay off his wife, you'll shut his yap.
And as for Wilder…" his voice trails.
Duke says, "He'll go to New South Wales."

"And as for your strained married life
You'd best patch things up with your wife.
I've one question, how'd Hayes's steeds
Leave bovine tracks upon the weeds?"

His Grace explains this in a trice.
"It is a medieval device
If my private museum you'd browse
There's horseshoes shaped like hooves of cows."

Holmes replies, "Most interesting!
Before I go, there's one more thing…
My fee's six thousand pounds, by heck!"
The Duke gulps. "Will you take a check?"

BLACK PETER

Watson exclaims, "Sherlock, look here!
What were you doing with that spear?"
Holmes says, "The butcher's. Nothing big.
I tried to run it through a pig.

Don't gape like I've gone off my head.
The piggy was already dead
My arms are strong, but fiddlesticks!
The pig I just could not transfix!"

The spear-tip barely made a dent
I learned from this experiment.
To emulate some mur'drous goon
Skewered a man with a harpoon."

An inspector calls– there's a knock!
Stanley Hopkins to see Sherlock!
"Holmes, please don't be sedentary
Find who harpooned Peter Carey!"

The clues add to the mystery
Tobacco-pouch lettered "P.C."
But Carey didn't smoke– he drank.
He'd extra money in the bank.

The killer's strength matched Hercules.
It seems missing securities
May form the motive for the crime."
Holmes says, "Watson, please lend your time!"

They search the scene, the room's ransacked
They catch a prowler in the act.
Hopkins exclaims, "We've got our man!"
It is John Hopley Neligan.

John claims, "I didn't kill Carey!
My father was a banker, he

Grabbed a bunch of securities
And vanished sailing on the seas

Dad's fate's unknown and can't be told
Lately some stocks of his were sold."
Hopkins sees bloodstains on John's book
And shouts, "I arrest you, you crook!"

"Hopkins has disappointed me,"
Holmes says, "Alternatives I see.
Neligan's got a frail physique
His puny arms are just too weak."

Holmes gathers up a few more clues
And calls sailors for interviews.
Patrick Cairns comes, he's got huge fists.
Holmes slaps the handcuffs on his wrists.

Upon the floor Holmes and Cairns rolled
(The breakfast eggs have gotten cold.)
Watson pulls out his revolver
Holmes says that Cairns' the murderer!

Hopkins is stunned– his face is red.
"I'm the pupil, you teach," he said.
Holmes smiles. "Learn from experience."
Now Cairns contributes his two cents.

"I killed Peter, can't be denied
I swear that it was justified!
The man came at me with a knife
I grabbed the harpoon, took his life.

Carey killed Nelligan senior
The stocks and bonds he did secure
I swear the man had lost his mind!
I left my tobacco behind.

I grabbed the bonds and ran away

The law should give me thanks, I say."
"Set poor Nelligan free today!"
Holmes and Watson head to Norway.

CHARLES AUGUSTUS MILVERTON

The worst man in all of London
Was Charles Augustus Milverton
Who Holmes once rightly compared to
A deadly serpent from the zoo.

For blackmail was Milverton's trade
Thousands of pounds his victims paid.
No one knew where his grip might fall
His name made scores of faces pall.

He paid top pound for documents
That could humiliate rich gents.
No one hit back at Milverton
He's cunning as the Evil One.

Lady Blackwell seeks Holmes' aid.
Charles Milverton wants to be paid
Seven thousand pounds right away
Or else he'll show her fiancé.

Some letters– sprightly, indiscreet–
They're for sale if the girl can meet
The ludicrously massive price
Set by this man who is not nice.

Holmes and Milverton then parlay
For Lady Blackwell cannot pay
The amount Milverton demands
To not cancel the marriage banns.

But Milverton will not relent.
He lowers his price not one cent.
He bids "good-day," doesn't look back.
So Holmes must try a different tack.

Sherlock then dons a keen disguise
As a young plumber, who espies

Upon Milverton, having made
The acquaintance of his house-maid.

Using all his charm and powers
Holmes studies Appledore Towers
(Milverton's home). One splendid night
The case's endgame is in sight.

"Tonight, dear Watson," Sherlock swore,
"I mean to burgle Appledore."
This statement sure makes Watson shake.
"Think twice, Holmes, please, for Heaven's sake!"

Holmes smiles. "Watson, silence your voice.
Milverton has left me no choice
No other option's qualified.
It *is* morally justified.

Lady Blackwell has one more day
And you know that she cannot pay."
Doc Watson's conscience writhes and twists.
"All right then, Holmes, I will assist."

At first Holmes balks, then says, "Well, well!
We two just might share the same cell."
The pair prepares for that night's tasks
And Watson makes some black silk masks.

Around midnight they make their way
To Appledore, and come what may
They break inside! And soon the gents
Find all the blackmail evidence!

Before the letters they can snatch
The doorknob turns, the lock does catch.
Just when capture does seem certain
The pair hide behind the curtain.

Milverton enters, takes a chair

And after a little while there
Comes a woman wearing a veil
Charles thinks she's come to talk blackmail.

She shouts "You have ruined my life!
I was happy to be the wife
Of a great man, and then you sent
My secrets to that noble gent."

"My husband wept, my husband cried,
He broke his gallant heart and died.
I wasn't quite the best of wives
But you will ruin no more lives."

"Take that, you stinking, filthy rat!
And that! And that! And that! And that!
She pumps Milverton full of lead.
"You've done me!" The blackmailer's dead!

Before the shooter flees the place
She grinds her foot into his face.
Next moment, Holmes grabs all the cache
Of letters, and burns them to ash.

Their mission is accomplished! Yay!
The duo make their getaway.
Although before they quite escape
A witness observes Watson's shape.

Next day Lestrade knocks on the door.
"A man was shot at Appledore
The victim's name was Milverton
He was quite a son of a gun.

Two culprits ran fast from the place
The undergardener saw one face
A strongly built man, a square jaw,
A moustache hangs upon his maw."

Holmes shrugs. "That's a poor description.
Those words completely fit Watson!"
"That's true," laughs Lestrade, "That's not great.
So will you please investigate?"

Holmes sighs. "I cannot help, Lestrade,
That Milverton was quite a bad
Fellow who specialized in crime
The law can't touch most of the time.

Don't argue! I've made up my mind!
Charles Milverton was so unkind
My sympathies are with the men
Who shot him! Good day to you, then!"

THE SIX NAPOLEONS

Sherlock has got a bizarre case
Who smashed the little corporal's face?
Some vandal's behavior disgusts
He's going around smashing busts!

For at Morse Hudson's knick-knack shop
A bust was crushed! He called a cop
Two Napoleon busts were bought
By the good doctor Barnicot.

Someone destroyed the statues good.
They're smashed to atoms where they stood.
Lestrade asks, "Could it be someone
Who really hates Napoleon?"

"Pish-tosh!" says Holmes. "That just won't do!
This case won't be my Waterloo!
The affair seems oddly trifling
Though great crimes start unpromising."

Next morning there's a graver turn
From Lestrade Holmes and Watson learn
Horace Harker's bust's been destroyed.
A John Doe's stabbed in the hyoid.

Holmes searches for a suspect's name
"It's Beppo!" Morse Hudson exclaims.
"He worked for me until last week
Did anarchists this havoc wreak?"

Soon Holmes discerns the killer's tricks
The busts were from a batch of six!
The fifth's bought by Josiah Brown.
Our heroes go to Chiswick town.

Outside Brown's house Holmes and friends wait.
A burglar stands aside the gate.

He's got Brown's bust– he smashes it!
Lestrade arrests the mad misfit.

"We've caught Beppo!" Lestrade holds the con.
"Sherlock, just what is going on?"
Holmes says, "It's too late to explain.
I need more time to wrack my brain."

Next evening at 221B
Mr. Sandeford arrives, he
Has brought the sixth bust, yes he did!
Sherlock purchases it for ten quid.

Holmes tightly grips his riding-crop
And gives the bust a mighty *WHOP!*
He searches the pieces– "Aha!
The black pearl of the Borgias!"

Here's what happened– a year ago
The pearl was stolen by Beppo.
The cops followed– Beppo ran fast,
Hid the pearl in a plaster cast.

He was sent to jail for a year
Then he searched for the nacre sphere.
He learned who bought Napoleons
Tracked down and smashed them one by one.

The murdered man was dogging him
(The reason for the killing's grim.)
Lestrade smiles "There's no policeman
Who wouldn't want to shake your hand."

THE THREE STUDENTS

Holmes and Watson go back to school.
Someone's cheating and that's not cool.
A scholarship is on the line.
Lecturer Soames's not feeling fine.

"To win, students must translate Greek,
I left forms out, one took a peek.
While I was gone, brief time elapsed
My servant Bannister collapsed.

Only three men could've done it.
McLaren is a lazy twit.
Daulat Ras is a quiet sort.
And young Gilchrist is good at sport.

They interview all three that night.
Gilchrist is friendly and polite
Daulat is in a nervous mood
And McLaren is downright rude.

Holmes finds bits of mud, shards of wood.
Next morning Holmes is feeling good.
He has been up since six A.M.
And now a cheater he'll condemn.

'Twas Gilchrist who peeked at the sheets,
He left behind mud from his cleats
A further clue was your tall height."
Gilchrist confesses, "You are right.

I wandered in, what did I find?
The test! Took notes, left gloves behind.
Bannister used to work for me
Hid the gloves so Soames wouldn't see.

Bannister, loyal through villainage
Chastised my unfair advantage.

I'll mend my ways, I'll leave uni,
South African police for me!"

Holmes smiles. "Now that this case is past
Watson and I need our breakfast.
Your future's bright despite your lies.
You've fallen low, now you must rise."

THE GOLDEN PINCE-NEZ

On a blustery, windy night
Hopkins asks, "Holmes! Please shed some light!
A man's dead– no one wished him harm.
The home of Professor Coram
Is the scene of this baffling case.
The house is called Yoxley Old Place.
Coram's writing a learned book
And a secretary he took
Inside his home– Willoughby Smith–
(I'll cut straight to the chase forthwith.)

A maid named Susan Tarlton found
Willoughby lying on the ground.
He had been stabbed once in the neck
And when Susan bent down to check
Mister Smith's pulse, suddenly he
Gasped "The professor… it was she."
The poor young man then fell back dead!
The housekeeper rushed to the bed
Of the professor, who's too weak
To stand, or do much more than speak.

(Whoever made Willoughby bleed
Coram could not have done the deed.)
Our heroes hurry to the scene.
Holmes looks with eyes sparkling and keen.
He talks with Coram, his eyes flash
(Holmes drops lots of cigarette ash.)
Housekeeper's got another clue–
Coram's eating enough for two!
Back at the professor's chamber
Holmes says, "I've solved the case, monsieur!

I scattered ashes on your floor
Clearly there is a secret door.
Behind the bookcase you will find
The killer, a woman half-blind.

I do not think she meant to slay
Your secretary yesterday.
She is not from the British Isles.
She broke in here to search your files.
You know she's here, she stayed all night
A woman rushes out: "You're right!"

"Madam," says Holmes, "You're far from well."
"Listen!" she cries, "I've much to tell.
I killed that man– didn't mean to–"
(Coram gasps, "Anna, God bless you!")
"I'm Coram's wife– we're Russian-born.
We were nihilists, oaths were sworn.
He sold me out, plus all our friends.
He profited for selfish ends.
My friend Alexis was guiltless
But in Siberia he rests.

My husband's perfidy's to blame.
These letters clear Alex's name.
Once I grabbed them, poor Smith attacked.
I found my spouse, forced him to act.
He hid me out of fear, not love.
These are this case's facts thereof.
Now take these papers– please don't wait–
Straight to the Russian Consulate.
I've drunk this phial, too late for me
Please hurry to the embassy!"

THE MISSING THREE-QUARTER

As Watson notes in his forward,
It's dangerous when Sherlock's bored.
Unless the sleuth can stretch his brain,
From bad habits he can't abstain.
A telegram ends inaction:
MISSING THREE-QUARTER– OVERTON.

This weird message, it Holmes confounds
Into their home an athlete bounds
Cyril Overton plays rugby
He's a student at Trinity.
His pal Godfrey Staunton is gone,
"He is the hinge the team turns on."

Holmes isn't well-informed of sports,
But his help Overton exhorts.
Holmes takes the missing person case
He starts asking questions apace.
"Now, who is Staunton's next of kin?"
"An uncle, sir, to his chagrin."

Lord Mount-James is a dreadful lout,
He's stingy, eighty, wracked by gout.
Godfrey is Lord Mount-James' heir
The miser is a millionaire.
Lord Mount-James sees no good value
In paying to find his nephew.

Sherlock searches Overton's rooms.
Upon a helpful clue he zooms.
A blotting-pad scrap– not opaque
It reads, "Stand by us for God's sake!"
A telegram speeds things along
It leads them to Doctor Armstrong.

Holmes asks Armstrong about Godfrey,
The doc snaps, "Get away from me!

Holmes cannot get a word in, so
He has to trail the medico.
Armstrong rides off with reckless speed
Holmes sprays his wheels with aniseed.

Pompey the draghound's on the scent!
Across the town they track the gent.
At a country cottage they find
Armstrong, who says something unkind
Holmes changes Armstrong's attitude.
The chastened doc shows gratitude.

"There's been no crime, as all can see
'Tis just a simple tragedy.
Not long ago young Staunton wed
A nice, but poor girl," Armstrong said.
"His uncle would flip if he knew
And disinherit his nephew.

His dear wife just got awfully sick,
Staunton rushed to her, she went quick."
With the facts in his possession
Holmes promises full discretion.
Holmes and Watson then take their leave
Allowing poor Staunton to grieve.

THE ABBEY GRANGE

"Come Watson, come! The game's afoot!
Stanley Hopkins wants my input
A home invasion, very strange
A murder at the Abbey Grange."

Our duo arrive at a hall
The home of Eustace Brackenstall.
He died from a blow to the face
(The poker from the fireplace.)

They then meet Mary Brackenstall
Upon the sofa she does sprawl.
"Limit your questions! Make them quick!
This situation makes me sick.

Though seemingly a handsome hunk
My husband was a nasty drunk.
Our marriage was a horrid blight.
Now I'll tell you about last night.

After the stroke of eleven
In burst three power'fly built men
I was knocked out, then gagged and bound
My spouse was hit– fell to the ground.

I can't say more!" the lady swears
Her loyal maid helps her go upstairs.
Hopkins says, "The killers will hang!
It must have been the Randall gang."

Holmes looks around, he spots a clue
Wine's opened by a knife's corkscrew
Beeswing's in one, not three, wine-cups
The bell-rope tied the lady up

The bell-rope's unevenly frayed
"Bring back the lady and her maid!"

Holmes says, "Ma'am, I know you lie
You are covering for some guy

I beg you, tell the truth! Be frank!
I'll earn your trust, and me you'll thank."
Lady Brackenstall mumbles, "No.
I have told you all that I know."
Holmes shrugs, he leaves, he asks around
Soon sailor Jack Crocker is found
Sherlock says, "Talk! And please speak true
Play tricks with me and I'll crush you."

"I'll chance it, Sherlock," Crocker cried.
"T'was by my hand Brackenstall died.
I met Mary before she wed.
I loved her, she chose him instead.
Recently I saw them again.
Her husband was the worst of men.
He smacked her face, made my blood boil.
We fought, he fell upon the soil.

A fake story my mind conceives:
We'll blame his killing on three thieves!
A burglary I had to fake
I threw some silver in the lake.
And that's the whole truth Sherlock, heck
Even if it costs me my neck."
"What say you, Watson?" Holmes queries
"Will you please serve as the jury?"

"I vote not guilty!" Watson cried.
"Justifiable homicide!"
Holmes says "*Vox populi, vox dei*
You may go, you are safe from me!"

THE SECOND STAIN

A client comes (a common trope.)
It's the Right Hon. Trelawney Hope
Along with the two-time Premier
Illustrious Lord Bellinger.

A document has disappeared
Without it global war is feared.
A silly king was indiscreet.
The clients beg at Holmes' feet.

The letter was locked in a box
Its reveal would inflame war hawks.
The letter was in there last night
But it was gone by morning light.

The clients skimp on the details
"You're wasting my time!" Sherlock rails.
They spill their guts, the odds are bleak
War's expected by end of week.

"The situation is desperate
No better way to approach it"
Holmes thinks. "Three spies could play this game…
Lucas, Oberstein, one more name…

La Rothiere! I'll see them all!"
"On Lucas you simply can't call,"
Says Watson, "He's been killed at home!"
Sherlock turns pale as Styrofoam.

"Somebody stabbed him in the chest."
Mrs. Hudson brings in a guest.
It's lovely Lady Hilda Hope
Whose speaking voice is soft as soap.

"Was my husband here?" "Yes he was."
"I suppose that he has come because

Of a stolen secret paper?"
It's secret, so Holmes can't tell her.

"Don't tell him I was here!" she cries
And out the door Lady Hope flies.
Though it's surprising, Scotland Yard
Solves the murder– it wasn't hard.

Lucas's lover felt jealousy
Stabbed him, and she fled to Paree.
But there's still one big question mark
So they go to Westminster Park.

Lestrade greets them "See that carpet?
It's bloodied there. The stain is set.
It should have seeped down to the floor.
Look at the wood! No trace of gore!

But come with me across the room!"
He lifts the rug and drops the boom.
A second bloodstain has been found!
Someone turned the carpet around!

Holmes slyly sends Lestrade away.
He checks the floor without delay
And finds a hole beneath a board!
It's where something secret was stored.

There's nothing there, Holmes asks the guard
"You see the woman on this card?"
"Yes, sir!" A flush comes to his cheek.
"I let her in to have a peek."

At this news Holmes' spirits soar.
"Hip hip hooray! There'll be no war!"
They rush away to the Hope house
To speak to the diplomat's spouse.

Soon as they cross the welcome mat

Hilda acts like a stuck-up brat
Holmes brushes off her rudeness. "Look–
Give me the paper that you took."

"You insult me, sir!" Hilda shouts.
"Our butler here will show you out!"
Watson is impressed by her verve
She's getting on Sherlock's last nerve.

"You saw Lucas, can't be denied
Your photo was identified
Cut out this stupid song and dance
Be frank with me– it's your last chance."

Hilda's bravado disappears
She hits the floor, breaks down in tears
Holmes' face is as hard as chrome
"Talk fast before your spouse gets home!"

She whips the letter from her sock
And hands it over to Sherlock.
"I presume that you have the key
Bring the dispatch-box straight to me!"

He shoves the letter back inside
Then questions the now-sobbing bride
"A letter from my callow youth
Was used for blackmail– that's the truth!

Lucas demanded the letter
What else could I have done better?"
Holmes rolls his eyes. "You should have told
Your husband– he treats you like gold."

Hilda breaks down, "I was afraid!
With the paper Lucas was paid
But after he gave me my note
That woman broke in and she smote

Him down with that knife, and I ran.
Then even more troubles began.
I didn't know how sensitive
The letter was– I swear I'd give

My right arm to take it all back.
I know I am no Brainiac.
I ran back, seized the envelope–"
Through the door walks Trelawney Hope.

The Prime Minister is with him.
"Holmes! Any luck? The time grows slim."
Sherlock's words cut right through the gloom.
"The letter never left your room."

Hope thinks that Sherlock Holmes has flipped
But from the box the letter's ripped
"How did you know? It's all a blur!"
"I knew it was nowhere else, sir."

THE VALLEY OF FEAR

Sherlock and Watson try to crack
A cipher with an almanac.
Moriarty's behind the code
Holmes is in cryptographer mode.

Soon the translated note is shown:
DANGER SOON– DOUGLAS – BIRLSTONE.
Before the meaning is deduced
DI MacDonald's introduced.

"I need your help," MacDonald said,
"Douglas of Birlstone House is dead!"
Holmes can't leave this mystery unsolved
He's sure Moriarty's involved.

Our duo hurries to Sussex.
The puzzle really does perplex.
Douglas has been fatally shot.
His head's reduced to nearly naught.

One point Sherlock is quick to note
It would be hard to cross the moat.
They try to soothe Douglas' bride
His death cannot be suicide.

Another point's sure to linger
Two rings were on the man's finger.
One ring was stolen post attack
One was removed… but then put back!

Cecil Barker's Douglas's friend.
He was staying for the weekend.
When asked who fired the big bang
Barker suggests a U.S. gang.

A phrase Mrs. Douglas did hear
Her spouse said "The Valley of Fear."

What does it mean? She cannot tell.
Also missing is one dumb-bell.

The wife and Barker ask Watson
"If we tell you who held the gun
Do you think Holmes could let it go?
And make sure no one else would know?"

"No deal!" says Holmes. "I'd rather die!
I know the tale they told's a lie!"
Sherlock flinches, as if in pain
"I think I've softening of the brain!"

Another clue upon the list:
There's an American cyclist
In town but he has disappeared.
Now towards the truth Sherlock is steered.

He sets a trap, gets Barker's goat.
A bundle's fished out of the moat
Weighed down by the missing dumb-bell.
The solution it's time to tell.

Douglas lives! He wasn't whacked!
A hit man came and he attacked!
The gunshot struck the other's face.
Douglas thought he could take his place.

The whole point of the wedding-band
Is that it won't come off his hand.
This was a case of self-defense,
But now, if you won't take offense

We'll fast-forward right to the end.
A flashback scene Conan Doyle penned
Of Douglas and the Pinkertons
He faces Scowrers and he runs.

It's not that bad, but then again

Without Sherlock and Watson then
There's no panache, no sense of heart
What say we all just skip this part?

Without our buddies it's a slog!
So cut right to the epilogue.
The Douglases are on the run.
To the dismay of everyone

Jack Douglas has fell off the ship!
An accident? Don't be a drip.
Moriarty's behind this crime.
But Holmes will beat him– give him time!

WISTERIA LODGE

Sherlock Holmes looks up from his desk
"Watson? How'd you define "grotesque?""
"Perhaps "strange" or "remarkable?""
"I'd say "tragic" and "terrible.""

Read this– I'VE FACED AN ODD BURLESQUE
LAST NIGHT'S ADVENTURES WERE GROTESQUE
MAY I CONSULT YOU? ECCLES, SCOTT
Watson, my interest has been caught!"

Into the room Scott Eccles flies
"I'm not a big fan of P.I.'s–"
The door opens, Mrs. Hudson
Ushers in Inspector Gregson.

"Sit back down, Eccles, please don't scram.
We traced you through your telegram.
Aloysius Garcia's dead
We want to know just why you fled."

"Mister Garcia was my friend.
He let me stay for the weekend.
The house and servants were gloomy.
Garcia's a cordial roomie.

I went to bed, when I awoke
The whole house was devoid of folk.
I asked myself "Is this a joke?"
That's all I know," Scott Eccles spoke.

"We believe you," Gregson replies.
"Your story has no hint of lies.
A twisty mystery still remains.
Oh, meet my pal Inspector Baynes."

Eccles says, "Holmes, please take my case!"
Sherlock replies, "The truth I'll chase!
Baynes, shall we all collaborate?"
And Baynes answers, "That would be great!"

Holmes then conducts some interviews.
They find some baffling grisly clues.
Baynes says, "I wish you luck, you pair!
I've a theory, but I won't share."

When Watson reads the papers, "Look!
Baines arrested Garcia's cook!"
Holmes confronts Baines, "I'll give you flak.
I don't think you're on the right track."

"You mean well," is Baines' reply.
There is a twinkle in his eye.
"I'll try my own way. It's my call."
Holmes grunts, "That man is set to fall."

Holmes digs around, and when he's done
He seeks a man named Henderson
Henderson's fled, the governess
Miss Burnett's still at the address

Baynes arrives. "Sherlock! Well done, you!"
We were on the same track, we two!
I know the cook is innocent.
I need to question Miss Burnett."

Miss Burnett has been mildly doped.
"We'll speak to her soon," Sherlock hoped.
"But who is the man who has gone?
What's the true name of Henderson?"

"Henderson is Don Murillo
Called the Tiger of San Pedro!
Central American tyrant
'Til revolution did displant."

At this point Miss Burnet revives
"Murillo snuffed out many lives
Including my darling husband.
Revenge Garcia and I planned.

Our thirst for justice was quite strong
But quickly everything went wrong.
Murillo's henchmen found my note
They planned to flee England by boat.

They killed Garcia, knocked out me,
By a miracle I got free!"
The story doesn't end that day.
Sadly, Murillo slipped away.

But not for long! Heaven forbid!
He gets his deserts in Madrid.
Holmes calls it "A chaotic case!
Truly grotesque from top to base!"

THE RED CIRCLE

Mrs. Warren has a lodger.
A most mysterious dodger
He pays a very hefty rent
And yet she never sees the gent.

When the lodger has a request
A very brief note is addressed
Like "SOAP," "MATCH," or "DAILY GAZETTE"
And those items the Warrens get.

Our duo sneak into the house.
They wait quietly as a mouse
And with a mirror's help they see
The lodger is a young lady!

Across the street, the window frame
Shows coded messages through flame.
One flash for "A," and two for "B"
The code's pattern should be easy.

What does the current message say?
 "A," "T," "T," "E," "N," "T," and "A."
Attenta! Italian! Beware!
What's going on with this affair?

They meet their old buddy Gregson.
They're introduced to Leverton
A quiet young American
Who's employed as a Pinkerton.

They cross the street, bust through a door
They find a body on the floor.
The corpse is Black Gorgiano
Holmes waves a light in the window.

Whoever killed the man knows knives.
Soon the lady lodger arrives.

Her name's Emilia Lucca.
She couldn't seek help from the law.

Emilia's husband tried to quit
A dark criminal syndicate.
The Red Circle is this gang's name
The Luccas ran, still bad guys came.
Emilia was hidden away
Their pursuer her spouse did slay.
The Luccas both were in the right
So Holmes heads off to Wagner night.

THE BRUCE-PARTINGTON PLANS

London is draped in opaque fog.
Sherlock is bored– life is a slog.
Mycroft's an unexpected guest
To talk about Cadogan West.

Holmes says to Watson, "By the way,
Do you know Mycroft's métier?"
Watson remembers, "At present
He's working for the government."

Holmes chuckles, "More than that, you see
At times the government is *he*.
Mycroft's position is unique
His memory is at its peak.

Be it taxes, warfare, or spies
All data he can synthesize.
Give him a moment, maybe three
He can dictate state policy."

Watson remembers– "West was found
Dead Tuesday on the Underground!"
Soon Mycroft enters with Lestrade.
"It seems our security's flawed.

The blueprints for a new machine–
The Bruce-Partington submarine–
Were stolen from the Woolwich vault.
The robbery must have been West's fault.

Our naval policy this warps
We found seven sheets on the corpse
Three more papers are sorely missed
Find them and make the honours list!"

Holmes smiles and gives his head a shake
"I play the game for its own sake.

This puzzle really is a tease.
Provide me with some more facts, please!"

Mycroft replies, "Sir James Walter
Supervises the saboteur
Clerk Sidney Johnson kept the key
What explanation can there be

Except that West stepped out of bounds?
The plans are worth ten thousand pounds!
Also, West and his fiancée
Were strolling when he ran away.

He wasn't seen again alive.
What treason did young West connive?
And where are the rest of the plans?
Have they been sold to foreign lands?"

Our duo runs– there's not much time.
They check out the scenes of the crime.
Holmes forms a theory with his brain.
West fell off the roof of a train!

He was killed elsewhere, thrown atop
A train-car, at a sudden stop
His corpse was thrown onto the ground
That's why no train-ticket was found!

They're seriously not playing games
They grab a cab to see Sir James.
Too late! He's dead! Causes not clear.
Colonel Valentine sheds a tear.

"The scandal broke my brother's heart!"
With no new clues our friends depart.
They question West's fiancée Vi.
"Cadogan wouldn't steal or lie!"

Holmes says, "Go on, Miss Westbury."

"He deplored lax security.
He was worried– don't know the cause
But he would not break any laws!"

Sidney Johnson informs the pair,
"The submarine could change warfare!"
Holmes asks, "Why would the plans West seize
When he could simply make copies?"

They ask Mycroft "Which foreign spies
Could sell off this top-secret prize?"
"There's LaRothière, who is scum
And Mayer's sneaky as they come

And finally there's Oberstein
He just left town, the dirty swine."
Holmes heads out, "We'll catch up tonight.
Watson, bring burglary tools, alright?"

They meet up at a shady place
Oberstein lived there, left no trace.
They hear the chugging of a train
This is the spot where West was slain!

Sherlock set out to catch the cad
Through a coded classified ad.
They see a worried man enter
It's Colonel Valentine Winter!

The Colonel copied James' keys,
Sold out his country, to appease
His creditors, with Oberstein
He stole plans for the submarine!

Cadogan caught them in the act
So Oberstein had poor West whacked.
The Colonel quakes with shame and fright
"Tell me how I can make this right!"

Holmes sets a trap, they tell the spy
There's more blueprints that he can buy.
They send a note, they sit and wait
Success! Oberstein takes the bait!

The villains are caught by the law
And Holmes meets Queen Victoria.
Her emerald pin is not refused
Clearly the Queen was most amused.

THE DYING DETECTIVE

Ms. Hudson calls– she's out of breath
"Sherlock is on the brink of death!
Three days, no food has passed his lips
By tonight he'll have cashed his chips.

It's far worse than the common flu
The only doc he'll see is you."
Watson comes– Holmes' face is drawn
His cheeks are flushed– "DON'T TOUCH ME, JOHN!

A rare disease known by the Dutch
Contagious, and it's spread by touch!
Keep your distance and all is well
Stay here 'til the six o'clock bell!"

The doorway Holmes closes and locks.
Watson spots a wee ivory box.
"Put it down this instant I say!
You could drive a patient cray-cray!"

Holmes babbles– Watson girds his loins
"John, redistribute all your coins
Oysters might conquer all the sea
Please light the gas half-on for me.

It's six o'clock, make your pace swift!
Now go and fetch Culverton Smith
Make sure he comes, but get back first!
Do it before I die of thirst!"

Smith really doesn't want to come.
Watson's powers of persuasion
Change Smith's mind– Watson hurries back
He hopes that Smith is not a quack.

Thankfully Sherlock's not yet dead.
"Quick, Watson! Hide behind the bed!"

Smith comes inside, takes off his coat.
He gives Sherlock an evil gloat.

"You're dying, Holmes, I have killed you.
I killed my nephew Victor, too.
The poisoned spring inside that box.
Will send you straight to Charon's docks.

So farewell, Holmes! This too shall pass.
Anything else?" "Turn up the gas."
Smith does, and sees that something's wrong.
Suddenly Holmes' voice is strong.

Inspector Morton then appears.
"Nice trap you've set!" Culverton sneers.
Lie as you like, you filthy boor,
My word is just as good as yours."

Holmes laughs, "Watson! I forgot you!
No longer one witness but two!"
Morton arrests the snarling Smith
And Sherlock has a snack forthwith.

"Some makeup, and no drink or food
Creates the ghastly face you viewed.
My pulse I couldn't let you take
You'd know at once my flu was fake.

We've closed a case, that's a big deal!
Let's eat a nice, nutritious meal!"

LADY FRANCES CARFAX

Where is Lady Frances Carfax?
Watson goes abroad to look.
Watson combs Switzerland for facts.
Did she hide or was she took?

Frances met a missionary
Known as Dr. Shlessinger.
Doc Shlessinger makes John wary.
Sherlock asks about his ear.

Watson questions Lady F's maid.
Seems a bearded man made threats.
Watson's attacked and nearly flayed
Thankfully some guy abets.

Not surprisingly, it's Sherlock!
"What a hash you've made of this!
Forgive me, I don't mean to mock
But you've really been remiss."

Our duo return to London
And learn about Shlessinger.
He is actually an ex-con
Named "Holy" Harry Peters.

They go after Harry Peters
Who's missing part of his ear
Also his wife Annie Fraser
Frances' fate provokes fear.

All their searches come to nothing
But her jewelry's being sold.
Peters buys a giant coffin
For a woman, very old.

Holmes' efforts are frustrated
And it makes him gnash his teeth.

In the coffin one woman's dead.
Could Frances be underneath?

Sherlock's right! The lady's inside!
And she's very close to death.
Respiration Doc Watson tried
'Til she finally draws breath.

Peters and wife wanted money
But were too squeamish to kill.
Now the crooks are on the runny
And Holmes has a chance to chill.

THE DEVIL'S FOOT

The case of the Cornish Horror
Is a very tragic tale
Featuring a great explorer
And a crime beyond the pale.

Holmes is on the verge of breakdown
So they leave to take a rest.
But a most perplexing murder
Puts his powers to the test.

When the vicar Mr. Roundhay
And his lodger Mortimer
Tregennis come over to say
That a strange crime did occur.

Mortimer has got three siblings
There's a sister and two bros.
Their fate will pull at your heartstrings.
And what harmed them? No one knows.

The four siblings were playing whist
And Mortimer returned home.
The brothers went around the twist
And the sister's dead as stone.

The explorer Leon Sterndale
Is a dear family friend.
He was just about to set sail
When the lady met her end.

The next day the vicar's frantic.
Mortimer is also dead.
Holmes finds powder on the lamp's wick
And the sleuth uses his head.

"This crime scene is awfully stuffy.
There is poison in the air.

This case really is a toughie.
Let's experiment– with care!"

Sherlock lights a lamp afire
Sprinkles powder in the blaze.
Their minds start to go haywire
Watson breaks out of his daze.

Watson saves himself and Sherlock
And Holmes offers sincere thanks.
"I must now make the killer talk
And make him pay for his pranks."

"Dr. Sterndale, I accuse you!
It was you who killed Morty!
His siblings Morty crazed and slew.
You didn't let him walk free!"

Sterndale cries, "You are a devil!
Morty's sister was my love.
I caught him and vowed to kill
For the law I am above.

This powder is rare and deadly
It is called the Devil's Foot.
Survive and face insanity.
It leaves lots of smoke and soot.

Morty killed his kin for money
And for that he had to pay.
I made him die like my honey
He deserved to face doomsday."

Holmes says, "Return to Africa
Bury yourself in your work.
Onto yourself you are a law
And your victim was a jerk."

HIS LAST BOW

We leave the age Victorian
And flash-forward to World War One.
Watson does not narrate this tale
Fragile peace is about to fail.

In the first scene we meet a dork,
A German spy, Heinrich Von Bork.
Von Bork thinks it a lovely treat
For England to fall in defeat.

To end diplomatic entente
He calls for agent Altamont.
They'll meet in a few hours hence
Altamont brings intelligence.

Altamont and Von Bork discuss
The growing espionage fuss.
At secret plans Bork takes a look
It's just a beekeeping textbook!

Von Bork blanches as white as chalk
Altamont is really Sherlock!
Two years he's been undercover!
Then enters a thickset chauffeur.

The chauffeur is Watson, of course.
They knock out Von Bork with some force.
They gag and bind the tied-up skunk
Then shove Von Bork in the car trunk.

Holmes tells Watson, "An east wind blows."
Watson says, "No, the warm sun glows."
Holmes smiles, "My spirits you assuage!
A fixed point in a changing age!

A cold, bitter wind comes, I bet
As never blew on England yet.

But it's God's own wind none the less
We'll be stronger after this mess."

THE ILLUSTRIOUS CLIENT

"Have you heard of Baron Gruner?"
"He's the Austrian murderer,"
Holmes replies to James Demery.
At this Colonel James laughs with glee.

"He killed his wife, that nasty gent
Made it look like an accident.
Holmes, what my friend wants you to do
Is prevent Gruner wedding two."

"Who is your friend?" "I cannot say."
"Too bad. I must bid you good-day."
James is upset. "Please hear the facts.
Gruner ruins those he attracts.

He can't wed Violet de Merville
A lovely girl of iron will
She is blindly in love with him
If they get hitched her future's grim."

Holmes sees Gruner, and he thinks that
The Baron's like a purring cat
Gruner sneers, "Back off, my dear man,
You can't succeed. Your work's barren.

With post-hypnotic suggestion
She won't listen to anyone
Be warned– if you try to thwart me
You might wind up an amputee."

Next Holmes meets Miss Kitty Winter
"I'll help you for me, not for her.
He ruined me, he crushed my soul
I want to crush that evil troll."

When Holmes sees Violet, she's ice-cold.
"All my love's secrets I've been told."
She won't listen, it's a pity.
(Violet's quite nasty to Kitty.)

Two days later danger balloons
Holmes is attacked by Gruner's goons.
"Watson if you want to help me
Brush up on Chinese pottery.

We'll stop Gruner if all goes well
Take this Ming pottery egg-shell.
This saucer he will want to see
I'll try to find his diary."

The Baron knows that something's odd.
He knows at once Watson's a fraud.
Holmes finds the journal– he runs out.
Gruner gives chase– he gives a shout!

Kitty Winter's entered the place
She threw vitriol in his face!
Kitty runs away through the yard
The Baron is forever scarred.

It's burned his eyes, also his hair.
"The pain is more than I can bear!"
Says Holmes with a humourless grin
"He's paid the wages of his sin!

We'll show this book to Violet
The wedding's off now, you can bet
This diary will crush her trust
It records all his crime and lust."

Violet dumps the Baron that night
And Kitty's punishment is light.
Of arresting Holmes there was talk
But he's not yet stood in the dock.

THE BLANCHED SOLDIER

Upon reading this tale fans say,
"Where's Watson? Is he here today?"
Alas, the doctor's MIA
Selfishly wed and gone away.

It makes a distinct change of pace
To see Sherlock narrate this case:
A conundrum that's very odd
Brought by a man named James M. Dodd.

"Help me, Holmes!" is James Dodd's plea.
"You have to solve the mystery
My war buddy, Godfrey Emsworth
Has vanished off the face of Earth.

I went to see his family
His dad was acting real shady
He said Godfrey was out of town
But with an odd sinister frown.

The Emsworths acted really weird.
Dad was peeved, Mom was a–feared.
The nervous aged butler said,
"I wish to God Godfrey was dead!"

Was I the victim of a con?
No one would say what's going on!
I'd gotten quite peeved at my host
And then I think I saw a ghost!

A man with a face white as snow
Appeared in my bedroom window.
When I investigated that,
"Get out of my house!" my host spat.

Holmes, something's happened to my friend!
I fear he's come to some bad end.

His parents are up to no good.
So look into this, if you would?"

Holmes asks some questions, and first chance
He gets, he goes to Emsworth Manse.
When Dodd and Holmes Emsworth espies,
He screams, "Get off the premises!"

Does this scare Sherlock? Heavens no!
Holmes is calm as billy-o.
He scribbles one word on a page
And this diffuses Emsworth's rage.

They are led to a tiny shack
A shocking sight sets them aback.
Dodd reunites with pal Godfrey
Who has contracted leprosy!

Mom and Dad weren't being mean
When they imposed this quarantine.
If anyone saw poor Godfrey
He'd be shipped to a colony!

Sherlock brings up one final twist.
He's called a dermatologist
Who checks out the piebald patient
And then announces that the gent

Who lies miserable in bed
Has been quite misdiagnosed!
It's not leprosy! Not at all!
It's unsightly but curable!

He's noninfectious! He'll be fine!
So he can leave this quarantine!
Ma Emsworth faints upon the floor–
That's it– there isn't any more.

THE MAZARIN STONE

This story's an unusual one
It is told in the third person.
A stolen diamond named The Crown
Is worth a hundred thousand pound.

Watson and the page Billy talk.
Into the room Sherlock does walk.
Holmes knows who stole the missing gem
But he cannot yet capture them.

Count Sylvius is suspect one.
The other's boxer Sam Merton
Holmes knows not the stone's location.
Sylvius just bought an air-gun.

Holmes gives Watson a task to do.
Billy shows in Sylvius, who
Upon seeing Holmes' profile
Tries to club him with a wild smile.

Holmes shouts, "No Count, do not break it!
That's a wax bust you're 'bout to hit!
It was made by Tavernier
It's quite a good likeness of me.

Count, I've got quite the file on you.
You're like plate-glass, I see right through
Your mind, so be reasonable
Give me the stone, then run like hell."

Sam Merton shows up, he's confused.
Holmes says, "You talk, I'll be excused."
He leaves, taking his violin
Soon there's the sound of fiddlin'

Count says, "Let's take the gem and scram!
We'll carve it up in Amsterdam."

"Sounds good!" says Sam, "Away I sneak!
The jewel– can I take one last peek?"

Sylvius pulls out the diamond.
Holmes grabs it out of the Count's hand!
(He slipped out through a second door
Displaced the wax bust on the floor.)

Why do they still hear the fiddle?
Gramophones are remarkable!
The police take the crooks away.
Billy enters with his card-tray.

Sherlock's guest is Lord Cantlemere.
A feeble figure, thin, austere.
Holmes plays a trick on the old goat
And slips the diamond in his coat.

Cantlemere stammers, blinks, and chokes.
Holmes laughs. "I love my little jokes!
Tell your friends I have solved the crime!
Call Ms. Hudson– it's dinnertime!"

THE THREE GABLES

"Please help!" says Mary Mayberley,
"My son Douglas died recently
Natural causes– not foul play.
A man came to my house today.

The name's Three Gables, he wanted
To buy it– would not be daunted.
When my lawyer read the fine print
I'd lose all my stuff– be left skint.

The buyer would get everything,
My clothes, my books, my wedding ring.
I did not like this sneaky clause–"
Holmes sees something and makes her pause.

The maid is list'ning at the door!
She's spying for someone not poor.
When Holmes coaxes the maid to tell
She screams at him, "See you in hell!"

"You need a guest to guard your home,"
Warns Holmes, "And now you need to comb
Through your son's bags from Italy
You just might find a clue or three."

The next day brings news far from nice
Mary ignored Holmes' advice.
She stayed alone– burglars broke in–
Took her son's stuff, to her chagrin.

One sheet of paper's left behind.
A novel's last page– it maligned
A woman as a source of strife.
The story has been drawn from life.

Before Holmes waltzes out the door
He adds two and two and gets four.

"What is your dream, Ms. Maberley?"
"I'd take a trip, the world I'd see."

Holmes says to John, "I've nosed around
Into Douglas's life and found
He dated Isadora Klein
A *femme fatale* with beauty fine."

Klein wishes to be left in peace.
Holmes asks, "Shall it be the police?"
She relents, lets the pair inside.
She is about to be a bride.

Isadora intends to wed
A duke, the lovelorn Douglas pled
For her to choose him, she said "no."
And this enraged her former beau.

Doug wrote a book about their fling.
He told her, she started freaking.
He died of heartbreak, Miss Klein flipped
She had to get that manuscript!

Her sneaky house-buying plan failed.
She turned to theft, she could be jailed.
Holmes says, "Pay up five thousand quid,
And no one will know what you did.

It goes to Mrs. Mayberley.
She'll get her global holiday."

THE SUSSEX VAMPIRE

Sherlock Holmes versus Dracula?
Not quite– this about a ma
Caught sucking blood from her son's neck.
When hearing of this, Holmes says, "Heck!

Vampires? Walking corpses? Sigh.
In my world no ghosts need apply."
"Look at this letter," says Watson.
"It's from a Robert Ferguson."

Bob is Watson's old rugby friend.
His family's not quite blended.
The son from wife one's just fifteen
With legs as weak as plasticine.

That brings us to wife number two
This woman was born in Peru
Twice she has struck the elder boy
When asked her reasons she was coy.

What's really got her husband's goat
Is licking blood off their son's throat!
Why harm the product of her womb?
They've locked her up inside her room.

The maid Delores watches her.
Holmes goes to Sussex to confer
And find clues to be analyzed
(The pet spaniel is paralyzed.)

Ferguson is at his wits' end
He says, "I cannot comprehend
Why my wife will not talk to me!"
Watson says, "I'll take a look-see."

When John sees Mrs. Ferguson
She's feverish and her face is dun.

"That fiend!" she cries clear as a bell.
"What shall I do with this devil?

No one can help me. All's destroyed!
Please bring to me my baby boy!"
Ferguson won't send her their kid.
"She'll drink his blood! I must forbid!"

Elder boy Jacky hugs and coos
Holmes examines the baby's wounds.
Sherlock says, "Now the case is done."
"Let's wrap this up. I've got to run."

They're in Mrs. Ferguson's room.
Holmes says, "I shall dispel your gloom.
I have figured out everything
We don't have to call Van Helsing.

Drinking blood? That I highly doubt.
Your wife was *sucking poison out!*
There's lots of weapons from Peru
When I saw poisoned darts I knew!

Jack tried to kill his little bro!
He's jealous, cruel, violent, emo.
He's weak, unhealthy, not too big
He made the dog a guinea-pig.

It's not Jack's first attempt to harm
So your wife whacked him on the arm.
Not telling you was not that smart
She thought the news would break your heart."

Mrs. Ferguson cries, "It's true!
I thought the truth would destroy you."
So Sussex Holmes and Watson quit.
The case? Let's put a stake through it.

THE THREE GARRIDEBS

Bizarre events comprise this story
Is it comedy or tragedy?
Judge for yourself– it *is* a mystery.
Three Garridebs in all!

One man lost freedom, one lost his mind
Watson lost blood when caught in a bind.
John Garrideb asks Sherlock to find
Three Garridebs total!

John Garrideb is heir in a will
But he cannot inherit until
He finds two more men who fit the bill
Three Garridebs in all!

Garrideb is an uncommon name
None in the U.S., and that's a shame
Must be adult males, can't be a dame.
Five million bucks– that's cool!

Holmes knows at once the story's a lie
Asks 'bout Doctor Starr– there's no such guy
Client says he knows him, being sly.
John Garrideb's a tool!

Nathan Garrideb enters the tale.
He's a collector, old and frail.
Never leaves his home, it's like a jail.
He rarely breaks this rule!

John Garrideb says he's found one more
Howard Garrideb– they don't need four.
Nathan must go, he heads out the door.
The money makes him drool!

Holmes realizes Howard is a hoax.
Homebody Nathan must be coaxed

To leave his house while someone pokes
'Round for some hidden jewel!

John Garrideb is an alias.
He's Killer Evans, cunning and crass.
Went to Holmes and lied as bold as brass.
What an amoral ghoul!

They catch Evans lifting up the floor.
Holmes and Watson rush to the trapdoor.
Then Evans whips out his revolver.
Watson is shot! How cruel!

Sherlock knocks Evans out in the fray!
"You are not hurt?" Watson hears him say.
His leg is grazed but he'll be okay!
He's hardy as a mule!

In the basement is a forger's den,
Evans had to drive away Nathan.
He'd sneak inside, grab the dough and then
He'd stuff a cash bag full!

Killer Evans is sent to prison.
Nathan's in a sanitarium.
Another win for Holmes and Watson.
Sherlock Holmes is no fool!

THOR BRIDGE

Neil Gibson, known as "The Gold King"
Ex-Senator, rich through mining.
He writes to Holmes– "I can't explain–
Miss Dunbar in jail can't remain!"

Mrs. Gibson's recently dead
A bullet wound upon her head.
The chief suspect's Miss Dunbar, who
Is set to be wife number two.

Miss Dunbar is the governess
It looks bad, but she won't confess.
A signed note says she was to meet.
Mrs. Gibson right down the street.

Sherlock asks Gibson when he comes,
"You and Miss Dunbar… more than chums?"
Gibson snaps, "No! Just solve the crime!"
Holmes says, "Don't lie! Don't waste my time!"

Gibson stomps out in a huge huff.
John asks "How'd you know?" Holmes says "Bluff!"
"I read the passion in his note.
Emotion's in the words he wrote."

Gibson returns quick as a wink,
"I love her– it's not what you think!
I tried to make her my side piece
But she said no to my caprice

I did not love my wife at all
But Grace Dunbar's a total doll."
Holmes groans, "You are a total roué"
I'll take this case for her, not you."

Though Gibson is a glob of slime
Holmes checks out the scene of the crime

Nothing makes sense. Just why would Grace
Leave the murder gun at her place?

The body was found at Thor Bridge
When Holmes examines the stone ridge
A chip's been knocked out of one rock
"Come, Watson! To the house we walk!"

The next thing Sherlock wants to see
Is Mr. Gibson's armory.
The murder weapon wasn't rare.
The pistol was half of a pair!

Sherlock interviews Miss Dunbar
"Why was the gun in your armoire?"
"I've no idea, sir. When I met
The mistress she was quite upset."

At last the truth Holmes does infer
"Come, Watson! Grab your revolver!"
Holmes asks a copper, "Can you bring
At least ten yards of sturdy string?"

A ball of twine is quickly found
And to one end the gun is bound.
The other end's tied to a stone
Holmes says, "Soon the truth will be known!"

Holmes takes the stone and dangles it
Over the Thor Bridge parapet.
Holmes walks to where the body lay
And cries out "Now for it, okay?"

He raises the gun to his head
Releases it, and then the thread
Pulls the weapon into the lake!
Another chip off the bridge breaks.

The truth is clear, it cannot hide.

Not murder, then, but suicide!
Mrs. Gibson had lost all face
And framed her hated rival Grace.

Holmes tells the policeman, "Now look,
You need to get a grappling-hook.
The other gun's there– can't be far.
Find it and release Miss Dunbar!"

THE CREEPING MAN

Heed this warning from Watson's lips:
May-December relationships
Can get messed up in a hurry
Like with Professor Presbury.

Presbury's engaged to Alice
And although it does sound callous
Some think it's a misdemeanor
That he's forty years her senior.

Now this Camford academic
Has been acting real erratic.
He's been crawling on all fours
And he's lurking at bedroom doors.

He has become furtive and sly.
A sinister glint's in his eye.
Now the Professor's pet dog Roy
Barks loud at him– and not for joy.

The Professor's behavior shocks.
He's got a little wooden box.
It seems to be of German make.
If you touch it your hand he'll break.

Presbury's character decays
Regularly every nine days.
His mad actions leave mouths agape
He climbs a trellis like an ape!

Holmes deduces, "Some shady drug
Is what makes him act like a thug."
While Presbury squats on the ground
He tortures poor Roy the wolf-hound.

In self-defense Roy snarls and bites.
Watson puts Presbury to rights

Holmes then opens the wooden box.
There is a note from some quack doc.

A serum made from monkey glands
Makes him creep on his knees and hands.
This supposed fountain of youth
Is what makes the prof act uncouth.

T'was Presbury's misguided plan
To make himself a younger man.
Holmes offers some advice that's sage:
Guys really need to act their age.

THE LION'S MANE

Retired and without Watson,
Sherlock must solve this case alone.
It involves teachers at a school
And danger in a lagoon pool.

The science teacher's wracked with pain
His last words are "the lion's mane!"
His back appears to have been flogged.
The authorities are befogged.

The math teacher's the chief suspect.
He mistreated the victim's pet
The headmaster claims they were friends
Despite their fights, they made amends.

Holmes meets the dead man's fiancée
Could the motive be jealousy?
Take a guess who was sweet on her
That's it! You're right! The math teacher!

The late man's dog, loyal and steadfast
Is found dead where his master passed!
Into reference books Sherlock dipped.
The math teacher looks sick and whipped.

Some brandy soothes the man's turmoil.
They dress his wounds with salad-oil.
He'll live– they can help him no more.
Holmes and his friends rush to the shore.

Holmes examines a verdant pool
And sees how nature can be cruel.
He's solved the case with his great brain.
Holmes shouts, "Behold the Lion's Mane!"

The water holds a jellyfish!
Its long tentacles writhe and swish.

It stung the teachers and the dog.
The men stare at the beast agog.

Holmes cries, "It's done mischief enough!
Help me push this rock off the bluff!"
The stone they shove falls with a slam.
The jellyfish is turned to jam!

THE VEILED LODGER

To South Brixton our heroes go
To help a Mrs. Merrilow.
Who came to Holmes and told a tale
Of a lodger who wears a veil.

Mrs. Ronder– that is her name
She hides her face– not out of shame
But 'cause it is mutilated
The sight of it sparks nameless dread.

The name "Ronder," it rings a bell
And to Watson Sherlock does tell
The tale of Ronder's Wild Beast Show
It is a story full of woe.

Rounder was killed by a lion
Who pounced on him, left him dying.
Close to him his wounded wife lied
"Coward! Coward! Coward!" she cried.

Holmes was wracked by deep suspicion
But couldn't wrap up his mission.
And now, years later, he will learn
Answers to the questions that burn.

When Mrs. Ronder they're meeting
After giving a quick greeting
Her veil hiding all expression
She starts to tell her confession.

Her husband's death's was a murder.
The circus strongman teamed with her
To kill her husband– such a swine!
And blame it on the big feline.

They club Ronder, open the cage,
The lion leaps out, filled with rage.

Her face the mad lion does flay
And then the strongman runs away.

So once she has divulged her tale,
The lady then lifts up her veil.
Oh, what a sad, horrible sight!
It makes one stay awake at night!

So mauled, so scarred, this grisly face
Almost makes Watson flee this place!
Holmes says with a stern little cough,
"Your life is not your own! Hands off!"

"I cannot bear it!" "Yes you can!
Suffer patiently! Be a man!"
And Mrs. Ronder, thinking twice
Decides to take Holmes' advice.

SHOSCOMBE OLD PLACE

Enter head trainer John Mason
He works for Robert Norberton .
He lives off sister Beatrice.
Mason thinks something's up with this.

"Sir Robert's debts reach to the sky.
He's got a colt that's really spry.
If Robert's pony wins the race
He'll be able to save his face.

Beatrice is now a recluse,
Avoids her horse, drinks tons of booze.
Robert? He doesn't sleep at night.
He sold his sister's dog– not right.

The master's messing with a crypt
One night into the dark he slipped.
He screamed, he lost all his sternness.
Oh! We found bones in the furnace."

In this business Holmes is poking
Did Robert murder his sibling?
Holmes gets Beatrice's spaniel
Who runs towards her carriage pell-mell.

The dog gets close– it runs away!
In the crypt a fresh corpse does lay.
Robert arrives, he waves a stick.
"Who is this corpse?" Holmes asks. "Talk quick!"

Robert confesses all he's done.
It is a tangled web he's spun.
Beatrice died naturally.
Her cause of death? It was dropsy.

But when she died, all her money
Went to her husband's family.

If her death had been made public
Creditors would swoop in real quick.

They'd seize his horse and all he owned
To recoup all the cash they loaned.
A plan! Pretend Beatrice lives!
The maid a fair performance gives.

The dog would know, so out it went
(The pup caught the maid by her scent.)
The body was stored in the tomb,
An old corpse was burned to make room.

He'd tell the truth after the race
When profits saved him from disgrace.
Holmes says, "The police must be told
I won't judge you." His tone is cold.

Robert's story ends happily.
His colt comes first in the Derby.
He pays his debts and all is grist
And the courts slap him on the wrist.

THE RETIRED COLOURMAN

Holmes meets Josiah Amberley
In a marriage December-May
Who got rich selling art supplies.
He comes to Holmes and wails and cries.

His heart's broken and it won't mend
His wife ran off his best friend.
The pal's name is Doc Ray Ernest
They left Josiah dispossessed.

Can Holmes track down the errant spouse?
Plus the cash taken from the house?
"Watson, can you take up the chase?
I'm tied up with another case."

When John returns he tries to paint
A picture of a cottage quaint.
"The Haven is the structure's name.
The neighbourhood's rather a shame

The brick streets are monotonous.
Weary suburb highways nonplus.
The high sun-baked wall's caked in dross.
Mottled with lichens, topped with moss."

Sherlock snaps at him severely,
"Watson! Cut out the poetry!"
A chastened John says "Amberley
Is a strange creature certainly.

His back is curved, bowed down by care
There's snaky locks of grizzled hair
His torso's strong, his legs are weak–"
"Left shoe wrinkled, right smooth," Holmes speaks.

"I didn't see that," says John, grim.
"You missed his artificial limb,"

Says Holmes, "Keep talking, don't stay mum!"
John notes, 'He's mad you didn't come.

Your praises I did try to sing
Amberley kept bellyaching
Once we had gotten acquainted
I saw the house had been painted.

Another odd thing I did see
A strange man was following me."
"Heavily moustached? Glasses grey?"
"Holmes, how'd you know? I did not say!"

Amberley bursts in like a ram.
"I have received a telegram!
The name "Elman" is on the page.
COME AT ONCE TO MY VICARAGE.

I do not think that I shall go."
"You must!" says Holmes. "You can't say "no!""
Watson travels with Amberley
At Little Purlington they see

The Reverend Elman, get his goat
He says he never sent the note.
Stunned, they return to The Haven
Where Holmes is waiting there for them.

Amberley screams, "What balderdash!
Who's that with grey glasses and 'stache?"
Holmes says, "He's Barker, an old chum
Now here's a question– don't keep mum

What did you do with the bodies?"
Amberley sinks down to his knees.
He tries to pop a poison pill
"No short cuts, sir! You need to chill!"

They take Amberley to the clink

Watson shouts, "I have tried to think
But I don't know what's going on!"
Holmes sighs, "His wife and her Don Juan

Were gassed to death inside this room
His jealousy assured their doom.
A sane and stable man he ain't
He covered the gas smell with paint.

To get a chance to search this place
I sent you on a wild goose chase.
I've proved Amberley took two lives
Watson, file this in our archives."

CONCLUSION

Is that all there is? Well, almost.
Before this book gives up the ghost
It would be remiss not to draw
Upon Holmes' apocrypha.

Two tales too short to fill handbills:
"The Field Bazaar" shows Holmes' skills.
He sees Watson and makes a claim
Connected to a cricket game.

Then in "How Watson Learned the Trick"
Watson sees Holmes and makes some slick
Deductions about his pal's next case
(Alas, Watson is far off base.)

So much for flash fiction! There's two
Longer stories that if read through
Closely suggest Holmes was involved
(A point that cannot be resolved.)

There's no mention of Holmes' name
Of course the man avoided fame.
"The Lost Special," I should explain,
Tells of a missing railway train.

In "The Man with the Watches" a
Man's killed on a train, yet the law
Can't catch the murderer and so…
Was Holmes called in? We do not know.

That is not where the matter lays.
Conan Doyle also wrote some plays!
"The Speckled Band" you've heard before
But not "Two Collaborators."

"The Crown Diamond" is better known
As the story "Mazarin Stone."

And before all my effort's spent:
"Holmes' Painful Predicament."

Is that the end? The answer's no.
Conan Doyle's work's exhausted, though.
Doyle stopped writing and that's a shame
But other authors joined the game.

One writer who I can't forget
Is the actor William Gillette
Who brought Holmes to life off the page
And played the sleuth upon the stage.

And Conan Doyle's son Adrian
Told John Dickson Carr "You're my man!
Collaborate on tales with me!"
So Holmes' *Exploits* came to be.

And Mark Twain wrote a parody
It's "A Double-Barreled Story."
P.G. Wodehouse went out to lunch
On a pastiche written for *Punch*.

Other new cases can be seen
Thanks to the great Ellery Queen.
You think that's it? You want to bet?
Well, how about Vincent Starett?

Also Monsignor Ronald Knox
And don't forget Edward D. Hoch.
Stephen Moffat and Mark Gatiss
Stephen Fry, Anthony Burgess.

Julian Symons, Bill Wilder
Also Dorothy L. Sayers.
On the radio, heard, not seen:
Anthony Boucher, Denis Green.

Nicholas Meyer's work begun

With *Seven Per-cent Solution.*
He wrote two more, put down his pen
Later he started up again.

Laurie R. King and Jô Soares
Also David Stuart Davies
Anthony Horowitz, Chris Chan
And there's Loren D. Estleman .

And Caleb Carr, Jeffrey Deaver
Michael Chabon, Colin Dexter
Also Kareem Abdul-Jabbar
Plus Kings Stephen and Laurie R.

H.F. Heard and Nancy Springer
Derrick and Brian Belanger
David Marcum and Mitch Cullin
Michael Hardwick and Rhys Bowen.

The mantle August Derleth dons
For pastiches with Solar Pons.
Margaret Walsh and Bonnie Macbird
Orlando Pearson and– my word!

Ken Ludwig and Leslie Bricusse
Edith Meiser stepped in Doyle's shoes.
And before we call it a day
We cannot forget Lyndsay Faye.

This list could go for pages yet
And if a name I did forget
Please do forgive the oversight
Edition Two will set it right.

What tales will form in someone's brain
Now Sherlock is public domain?
Holmes' adventures are not through
His next big case could be by you.

THE END?

www.ingramcontent.com/pod-product-compliance
Lightning Source LLC
Chambersburg PA
CBHW080743250626

47162CB00010B/3012